OTHER BOOKS BY SUSIE BRIGHT

Mommy's Little Girl:
On Sex, Motherhood, Porn, and Cherry Pie

Best American Erotica 1993–2004, editor

How to Write a Dirty Story

Full Exposure

Nothing But the Girl (with Jill Posener)

The Sexual State of the Union

Sexwise

Susie Bright's Sexual Reality

Susie Sexpert's Lesbian Sex World

Herotica I, II, & III, editor

A TOUCHSTONE BOOK

PUBLISHED BY SIMON & SCHUSTER   NEW YORK   LONDON   TORONTO   SYDNEY

Susie Bright presents

three
the
hard
way

Erotic Novellas

WILLIAM HARRISON

GREG BOYD

TSAURAH LITZKY

TOUCHSTONE
Rockefeller Center
1230 Avenue of the Americas
New York, NY 10020

TOUCHSTONE and colophon are registered trademarks
of Simon & Schuster, Inc.

For information regarding special discounts for bulk purchases,
please contact Simon & Schuster Special Sales at
1-800-456-6798 or business@simonandschuster.com

Manufactured in the United States of America

10   9   8   7   6   5   4   3   2   1

Library of Congress Cataloging-in-Publication Data

Susie Bright presents three the hard way : erotic novellas /
by William Harrison, Greg Boyd, Tsaurah Litzky.
        p.   cm.
    Contents: The motion of the ocean / Tsaurah Litzky—The widow /
Greg Boyd—Shadow of a man / William Harrison.
    1. Erotic stories, American.   I. Title: Three the hard way.
II. Litzky, Tsaurah. Motion of the ocean.   III. Boyd, Greg, 1957– Widow.
IV. Harrison, William, 1933– Shadow of a man.

PS648.E7S87   2004
813'.60803538—dc22   2004041769

ISBN 0-7432-4549-0

DEDICATED TO THE
MEMORY OF TOM O'CONNOR;
APRIL 12, 1950–NOVEMBER 6, 2003

contents

Introduction   xi

1   The Motion of the Ocean   TSAURAH LITZKY   1

2   The Widow   GREG BOYD   111

3   Shadow of a Man   WILLIAM HARRISON   173

Author Biographies   233

About the Editor   235

introduction

Get in, get out, don't linger.

It sounds like a pornographic maxim, but it's actually Raymond Carver's axiom about how to craft the perfect short story. Erotic literature, in our lifetimes, has usually fit his bill. It's short, all right. Sexy stories have typically been told in punch lines, bawdy tales, quickies from a raconteur. I've seen erotic anthologies that proposed to tell a story in under a hundred words, then under fifty. Erotic storytellers have beaten the devil, then the censor, and finally the clock.

There's an untold parable behind the quick and the hot. Sexual writing has suffered under a lot of shame, and that's made it difficult to thrive. In a great deal of America's publishing history, you had to be a beatnik or a pornographer to get your hands on any form of erotica, whether crude or existential.

A couple decades ago, when commercial literary publishers began to produce erotic volumes of their own, they did so with two caveats. First, the movement was led by women, who saw self-defined erotica as overdue emancipation. Secondly, the offerings were diverse, the essence of a variety pack. No one could predict what pieces would appeal or offend, so the book was full of surprises, and hopefully two or three would entice each reader. Appalled by the whore on page 38? Turn the page and maybe you'll appreciate the strange spinster on 39.

The "lots-of-variety, nothing-too-long" approach was successful. New male authors joined the female throng of nonapologists. New readers became erotically tolerant as long as you provided them with a diversity of subject and style in each package. It was either that, or you went the porno-niche route and published titles that indicated a single-minded focus: "My Best Friend's Horny Bisexual Wife." These titles are the very definition of seasoned pulp, but for self-evident reasons, they never were called literary. They relied on stock characters as much as stock titling.

Meanwhile, what did the authors think? Writers love short stories, it's part of our character. Not because we're lazy—writing an exceptional short story can kill you—but because the form is classic, demanding, and breathtaking when it works. It makes a big impact seem even bigger because it is accomplished with brevity.

Yet, with so many talented writers entertaining frank and original sexuality, why would longer-length stories *not* emerge? In the writers' mind, they certainly do. A few years ago, while editing an edition of *Best American Erotica*, I realized that I was receiving excellent manuscripts much longer than I could include in a normal anthology. Some of them were so good it was a shame they weren't novels in their own right.

I felt silly telling the author, "Dear Old Thing, Your story is delicious, and could easily be twice as long, but there simply isn't a publishing venue to accommodate it." Instead, I had to ask myself, "*Why not?*" Why can't we take a chance that someone has the chops to create an erotic story worth holding a novel's worth of attention?

The three novellas in this book do just that. Tsaurah Litzky, Greg Boyd, and William Harrison are all authors at the top of my list when it comes to prolific, uncorked inspiration. I met them in the course of my work on the *Best American Erotica* series. Harrison was suggested to me by a *B.A.E.* reader who spotted his work in the *Missouri Review*, a place that I was not searching to find erotica! Litzky came to me courtesy of Joe Maynard's Brooklyn zine, *Pink Pages*, which, in retrospect, divined some of the best erotic writers working today. And Greg Boyd is a seismic original of California bohemia, whom I first met when we performed on stage together. He had made up his body and costume into two distinct halves, one bearded, one not—one dark, one light. His performance was perfect erotic schizophrenia, and I made up my mind to read everything he ever put on paper. I felt the same way about Tsaurah and Bill, and none of them have ever disappointed me.

I didn't ask for a particular topic when I called my authors. I didn't say, "Give me virgins—no, dwarves—and I want it in Greece." What I wanted were characters and visions that went beyond fable-length proportions. I knew there was an erotic zeitgeist percolating, but it wasn't going to have a facile categorization.

When I received the final stories, I got my first picture of what it was all about: *Three the Hard Way.* Each story is led by mature protagonists, characters who go through a personal sea change—and not without a struggle. They aren't ingenues, and this isn't anyone's first time. They are actually antivirginal, a stake against superficiality. No spoon-feedings here, or games of "let's not and say we did."

My friend Jackie Strano came up with our very apt title. This is the terrain where authentic sexuality is more memorable than a quick tease. These three gave me a tussle and a surrender that was mercifully . . . drawn out. I lingered, and I loved it. I'll be grateful to them, always, for fulfilling my jumbo-size imagination.

Susie Bright
Spring 2004

the
motion
of the
ocean

Tsaurah Litzky

Dedicated to Sugartown

Bar Mitzvah Boy

feel I need to organize my life. I buy a loose-leaf photo album with enough plastic sleeves for three hundred pictures at the Weber's Job Lots for $4.99. I go home and take the cardboard box that holds my lifetime accumulation of photos out of the closet. I dump the photos out of the carton onto the kitchen table, rip the cellophane casing off the album, and sit down at the table. I am ready to begin.

The first picture I pick up is some thirty years old and crinkles around the edges. It was taken at the Remsen Heights Jewish Center in Canarsie, Brooklyn. The young teen version of my brother is standing between two couples. To his right stand my mother and father; to his left, my first husband, Stanley, and me. We are posed next to a table holding a big rectangular white cake. It is just possible to make out the words on the cake, *Happy Bar Mitzvah, Seymour,* and the miniature torah inscribed beneath.

My father stands to the far right in the picture. He is looking shiftily away from the rest of us out of the frame; perhaps he is looking over at his gambling buddies gathered around the bar. In the last year my father lost so much money at the track that my mother had to sell her mother's diamond engagement ring to cover the costs of this bar mitzvah. My mother stands next to him wearing a long silver dress. She is petite, exquisite, with a heart-shaped face and long almond eyes. She is looking calmly into the camera, smiling as if she is on twenty milligrams of Valium. But my mother does not believe in taking drugs. It is only her iron will, her determination that we appear a happy family, that is holding the smile on her face, holding the picture together. When I told her a month before the bar mitzvah that I was going to divorce Stanley, she said, "You never stick to anything, just like your father." Stanley and I are here for appearances. My mother didn't want to ruin my brother's bar mitzvah with the inevitable gossip that my solo appearance would provoke. Stanley and I agreed to attend as a couple.

I did not tell my mother how, right after our wedding, I discovered that Stanley had been having weekly trysts with Dennis, his biology teacher at NYU. I was trying to decide if I could possibly live with this when Stanley told me he wanted Dennis to move into the spare room in our apartment. I knew I had to divorce him. In the picture Stanley is standing on the far right. His arm is around my back; his chubby hand is around my waist. He has a doughy white face that looks something like a cream puff, suggesting the pastry chef he will eventually become. I am standing next to him with my arm around my brother, whom I adore. I have the same beehive hairdo as my mother. I am wearing a short, red, strapless cocktail dress that shows I have inherited her fine bone structure. My face is open in a painfully wide smile. I am glad the bar mitzvah is now three-quarters over, the dinner finished except for dessert and coffee. There remains at most another hour of dancing and then the cutting of the cake. No one in the picture knows that I have a secret.

I have also begun to have weekly trysts. Every Tuesday afternoon I rendezvous with Morrie Schreiber, the family accountant, at the Golden Gate Motel on Emmons Avenue. Morrie was in Korea, where he learned to like things that his wife, Glenda, won't do. For our afternoon of games he always gives me a hundred dollars. I am saving this money to pay for the divorce and also because I hope to go to Paris this summer at the end of my sophomore year at Brooklyn College. Morrie says that if I don't have enough he will give me the extra, but I don't want to take anything from him that I don't earn. Glenda was three years ahead of me in high school. I was a bookworm, a geek. She was a cheerleader who won the Aaron Copland Music Prize and a scholarship to the Boston Conservatory of Music. She turned down the scholarship to marry Morrie. Now she is a size fourteen and gives piano lessons in their home. My brother is one of her students. They are both here at the bar mitzvah. Morrie has been hovering over her, very solicitous. He and I do not look at each other.

Now we come to my brother, the center of the picture, Seymour, the Bar Mitzvah Boy, the mazel tov boychick. He is skinny as a string; he has not yet started to shoot up. He is still shorter than my mother and me; we both stand five-foot-two in our high heels. His flattop buzz cut reveals that he has a pointy head. His face is narrow, his eyes big and round. He will grow into a handsome man, but now he looks something like an ant except that he has my father's huge ears. The only parts of him that have started to grow are his hands, which jut out below the sleeves of his jacket, big as a pair of boxing gloves, and his feet, which are already size eleven. He is also smiling, but I don't know why. The band has been on a break.

They begin to play again, *"Bei Mir Bist du Schoen."* The music carries us out of the picture back into the party.

"How about you and me jitterbugging out there?" says my cousin Denise's husband.

His name is Vinnie. He grabs me and pulls me out to the dance floor.

"So how is married life?" says Vinnie. "Still the happy bride?" The official story is that Vinnie, who is Italian, sells cars for a Chrysler dealership in the Rego Park neighborhood where he grew up. In truth, we all know that he is a strong arm and that he works for the Giabruzzi family, collecting gambling debts. My cousin Denise, who is six years older than me, is eight months pregnant. She is seated with her mother, Lillian, at their table. They are both crocheting. They crochet everywhere they go.

"Married life is great, wonderful," I answer Vinnie.

"Well, if you ever get tired of that kosher salami, Cousin Vinnie's got a big piece of meat you'd die for."

I am shocked, horrified. "But Denise, but you—" I start to sputter.

"Listen college girl, wise up," he says. "If it's not gonna be you, it's gonna be someone else."

I tear myself out of his grip and run back to our table. I sit down and see that Stanley and my mother are dancing. My father is drinking with his gambling buddies at the bar, and my brother is seated with his friends at their table.

I watch him among his pals. He is the smallest one but the most animated, the most intelligent-looking. He is always moving around, always joking. All the boys have cigars. Seymour puts his unlit cigar in his mouth and pretends to suck on it, rolling his eyes. The sucking motion hollows his cheeks out. This makes his cheekbones more prominent. His face suddenly resembles mine, particularly as I glimpsed it last week in the mirror over the dresser opposite the bed in room 2B of the Golden Gate Motel.

Morrie is seated on the edge of the bed, his legs spread wide. All he's wearing are his white cotton T-shirt, his black socks, a gold Star of David around his neck, and his wedding ring. I know he would remove the wedding ring if I asked him, but I guess I don't care. His thick, stubby cock is in my mouth. I am trying to suck it deep into my throat. This effort hollows my cheeks and changes my face so I look Byzantine and exotic. I have learned that the more liquid I keep in my mouth, the easier the sucking.

Morrie always brings a small bottle of B&B in his briefcase for me. I always drink some before we start. If I bend my head back at a certain angle, his cock slides down my throat like Santa down a chimney—the Jewish Santa, that is. The Jewish Santa is skinnier than the Christian version. He looks like an Israeli commando. Morrie looks like an Israeli commando, too, when he takes off those thick glasses, and part of what he likes to do is order me around. He doesn't like to come when I'm sucking him. "That's enough," he will say sharply, and then, "Assume the position." I have been trained to say "Yes sir" in response. I then assume doggie position sideways on the bed so that my dangling tits—Morrie calls them my love jugs—will be visible in the mirror. He kneels behind me, between my spread legs. He always spits saliva on his palms. He rubs the saliva on his cock, then slowly, watching in the mirror, he inches his cock into my back hole. This is what he says Glenda won't let him do. I have come to like it, particularly when he reaches around in front of me and puts two fingers inside. He fingers me in such a way that I come when he does.

Someone taps me on the shoulder. I realize I have been so deeply immersed in my thoughts that I've forgotten where I am. Thinking about Morrie and me has gotten me wet. I can smell myself; I smell like Concord grape Passover wine. I cross my legs and look up to see Stanley standing above me, hand outstretched.

"Wanna dance, wifey?" he asks.

"Okay," I answer, and stand up. We take a place among the dancers and start to do the foxtrot to "Shine On, Harvest Moon." Over his shoulder I can still see my brother and his friends at the bar mitzvah table. They are no longer pretending to puff on cigars but are having a food fight, throwing the leftover dinner rolls at one another. I wonder if my brother has made out with a girl yet. I know he jacks off because two months ago he asked me to buy *Playboy*s for him with the money he makes washing cars. Now he has a small stack of *Playboy*s hidden under the box of toy soldiers in his closet. Stanley and I do another foxtrot, a mambo, then the cha-cha to Mickey and Sylvia's "Love Is Strange." "The perfect picture of young married happiness," I hear my aunt Millie say as she dances by with Uncle Arthur. The bandleader has just announced a hora. This brings more people out to the dance floor—the kids, the grandmas, and the old couples. We form a circle. My mother taps my arm and pulls me away from my place next to Stanley. "Come with me," she says.

She leads me to the side of the room away from the circle of dancers. "I can't find Seymour anywhere," she says. "I even asked Cousin Irving to look for him in the men's room, but he wasn't there. I have to find him; right after the hora is the cutting of the cake. Look, his friends are all dancing, but he's not there." I look around and don't see my brother. "I'd ask your father to help me look for him," my mother continues, "but he's so drunk he couldn't find his *shvantz*." I glance over to the bar and see my father standing among his cronies. Morrie is there, too, and my father has his arm over Morrie's shoulder and is talking right into his face. I look quickly away.

"Please help me find him," my mother says. "You look in the basement. I'm going to look outside the shul."

"Right," I say, and go out of the banquet room. I go down the long hall and take the stairs that lead to the basement.

There are several small classrooms in the basement where Haftorah lessons are taught that prepare boys for bar mitzvah. The classrooms are empty. I knock loudly on the door of the single bathroom. Then I stick my head inside and find it empty, too.

From the floor above I can hear the stamping feet and the bandleader singing, "*Ha-va-na-ra-na-na, vir mist ba ha.*" There are several unmarked doors farther down the corridor. "Seymour, Seymour," I call out, but get no answer. I go down the hall and open the first unmarked door. I find a little room with a big desk, a couple of chairs, a file cabinet.

The next door opens into a broom closet, filled with stacks of pails and shelves loaded with cleaning supplies. There, facing me, standing behind the mops, is my brother. His eyes are closed. He has the same look of intense pleasure on his face that he gets when he watches Bullwinkle cartoons. His tuxedo pants are down around his ankles, and he is not alone. Kneeling between his legs is Glenda Schreiber. Her broad bottom, covered by mint green silk organza, bobs up and down as she moves her head between his legs. She does not seem to have heard me open the door because her in-out, in-out rhythm continues uninterrupted. Not a single red hair has strayed from her ornate French twist, thanks no doubt to the glory of Spraynet. My brother opens his eyes; a look of fear comes over his face as he sees me. I love him so much at that moment. I place a finger against my lips to reassure him, point to an imaginary watch on my wrist and silently mouth the words *cutting the cake.* He nods his head. As quietly as possible, I shut the door.

At the top of the stairs, my mother rushes up to me. "Did you find him?" she whispers. I shook my head. "He wasn't outside, I even looked in the parking lot. Oh, where could he be?" she says, almost weeping. I tell her that he is probably around the corner sneaking a cigarette. "You know how kids his age start with that. Remember that time you caught me smoking in the backyard?" I said.

"I just don't like this," my mother sighs.

"Don't worry," I reassured her, "I'll tell the musicians to play 'Hava Nagila' again."

Out on the dance floor, the dancers are leaping and whirling about in a frenzy. They are led by my fifty-year-old, 250-pound cousin, Arlene. When I ask the bandleader to play the hora one more time, he says, "Okay, but don't blame me if she has a heart attack." I cut into line next to Stanley. I ignore his "Where have you been?" as I get into step—left-right kick, right-left kick. . . . Glenda comes into the room. A few minutes later, I see the back of my brother's little yarmulke'd head. My mother is grasping him firmly by the arm.

I stand next to my brother as he is cutting the cake. "So," I whisper into his ear, "was tonight the first time you became a man?" He cannot look at me; he looks down at his big feet.

"No comment," he mumbles.

———

I put the old picture back on the table. Eventually my father realized he was being a jerk. He managed to stop gambling and took up stamp collecting. Glenda and Morrie separated, and he became a

Hare Krishna. I don't know what happened to her. My brother grew up to be successful in business and a happy family man. After I divorced Stanley, I did go to Paris, and that began my journey out into the greater world. I no longer wear a beehive hairdo, but I am still a size three.

I decide this is the perfect snapshot with which to begin my album. I take the picture and slide it into the first plastic sleeve.

Sugartown

His fingers were like honey sap; wherever he touched, he left a sticky sweetness on my skin. After he was out the door, I liked to lie in bed and lick up and down my arms, then I'd bend my head and lick along the inside of my knees. He liked to put his fingers there, pull my thighs wide open and gaze into me. He would say my cunt was the eighth wonder of the world, then he would bend his fair head down between my legs, or take his cock out and give me some sugar. He never ran out of marshmallow milk. When he was around, it was always Sugartown.

His name was Leo, but I called him Lionheart because he was my conqueror. He was my conqueror, but he did not have to subdue me. I yielded, surrendered myself to him completely from the very first.

It started when he rang my bell on a cold November afternoon. He said he was in the neighborhood taking pictures, but I didn't believe him. I knew why he had come. He knew I wanted to see his cock; he had to know it, must have known it, from the way I always sought him out after my act. I'd go right up to him at the end of the bar where he stood scanning the crowd for troublemakers. I'd ask him for a cigarette, puffing my lips out to make them look more kissable. I could never keep from glancing down at his crotch, at the sturdy package visible beneath the fabric of his jeans.

I was so bold that first day. I had no idea what was in store for me.

"Why don't we just go into my bedroom and lie down?" I said, after we drank the coffee I had made. I wasn't ready for the ferocity with which he attacked me; I wasn't prepared for how roughly he threw me down on the bed. He shucked off my clothes without even kissing me first. He grabbed one of my breasts with his strong hand, pressing down with his palm, squeezing my flesh, hurting me. Then he took my other tit in his mouth and bit down sharply, chewing, mauling, teasing that little tit with his teeth, until, despite the pain, it became harder than a tenpenny nail.

It hurt so much, I didn't know why I wanted more and more. My loving nature suddenly changed, became wanton, deranged. He took that hand off my breast and stabbed two, three fingers into my cunt, transforming it into a desperate, hungry creature, a ravenous mouth. I spread my legs at a 90-degree angle to open myself even wider because I had to have all his fingers inside me.

Only after I came, after the searing sharp flame in the center of my body became undulating waves of rippling pleasure, did he take his fingers out. Then he peeled off his clothes, and finally, I got to see his cock.

It was a tremendous cock, a rock of a cock, a monster cock, a lollapalooza. It could have been the creation of some mischievous, ancient priapic god from a long time ago. It was too large for his slender frame. It belonged on a big stud bull. The thick red shaft meat was tied together with hard, yellow veins. The cockhead was fat, rubbery, and purple, a killer mushroom that might poison me with the first bite or mutate me into an Alice in Wonderland.

I did not have the chance to summon my courage and try a taste, because he just pulled open my knees in that way I would come to love, and rammed that nasty cock right into me. I thought it would rip me apart, but it slid in so easy, it was hand-in-glove from the start. I swung my legs up around his waist; and with all the strength in my cunt, I sucked that cock so deep into my womb that it tickled my eyes, making me cry ecstatic tears. His fat bull balls slapped the open crack of my ass as he rode me. I felt that monster cock draw back and tremble like it was getting ready to shoot, but I wasn't quite there. He knew just what to do. He jabbed a long, limber finger right up my yearning back hole and pushed me over the edge. We were falling, welded together by the fire between our legs. Our bodies were shooting sparks so hot that when we landed in a bubbling hot spring, it did not burn us.

Before he left, he put that rank finger in my mouth and I sucked it clean.

He started dropping by at least once a week. We learned to play all the different ways. I grew to love his incredible cock; it no longer seemed like an anomaly to me. Sometimes it was still hot red meat, but more often it was my special treat, my dessert. When I opened my mouth to suck it, it became my candy cane, my sugar pop.

Pomegranate Girl

It was a warm, fall evening. Lionheart, Percy, and I were on a magical mystery tour in sympathy with the Chicago Eight, who were going on trial in a few days. Besides, Lionheart had sold a painting and wanted to celebrate. He visited the Astro-Zen chemist in his basement apartment on Rivington Street. There he bought six capsules of the purest lysergic acid diethylamide mixed with super methamphetamine in a base of mescal extracted from the rare Madre de Dios plant. Higher than Mount Titicaca on two caps each, we bounced off the walls of Lionheart's room, dancing, whirling like Sufis and singing "Wild Thing."

Suddenly Percy stopped dancing and started screaming. Then he dropped to the floor, crawled under Lionheart's bed. "Klingons, Klingons," he yelled. "Take cover, they have zap guns!" We crawled under the bed, too; after a while we got him to calm down. We assured him that his dreadful visions were side effects of the drug, and that he would soon pass through the dark void and see the light of cosmic truth. Then we decided to go up to the Gristedes on Henry Street and get some walnuts. As seasoned psychedelic wan-

17

derers, we knew that the potassium in the walnuts would bring us down a little.

In the Gristedes, a grinning stock boy with Dracula teeth and exploding, lightning-bolt hair directed us to aisle five for the tinned walnuts, but we wanted the natural, in-the-shell kind. We wandered past paper goods, cleaning supplies, pet food until we found the produce department. As befit the hunters, Lionheart and Percy walked in front, while I, the gatherer, stayed behind.

We came to the walnuts, all piled in a bin. I scooped several handfuls into a plastic bag while Percy and Lionheart stood guard. Then Lionheart saw the pomegranates, stacked in a pyramid between the pears and persimmons. He walked over and picked one up. "This is your fruit," he said, holding it in front of me. "It's like you, a little bumpy." With his other hand he reached out and squeezed my tit, making me giggle. "But beautiful, too, and filled with ruby juice. You're a pomegranate girl," he added. Percy nodded his head.

"Wow," Percy said, "you got it, man, right on."

Lionheart slipped the pomegranate into the inside pocket of his lumber jacket, then he took the bag of walnuts from me and we went to the cash register. As he paid, Percy and I stood behind him, talking loudly about the Moody Blues to create a distraction.

We cracked the walnuts in our teeth and ate the meat as we walked down the street. We put the shells in our pockets to throw in the garbage later because we were good and decent citizens of the pious, pulsing, perpetual, perpetuating universe and we never littered.

When we got home, Lionheart put the pomegranate on the windowsill above his bed. Later, I could see it glistening scarlet red as I lay in the cradle that he and Percy made of their arms. While we watched, the tops of our heads floated up in wavy, frondlike shreds out the open window and up into the starry night sky. Lionheart said Percy was his best friend and I was his pomegranate girl. Percy said, "Wow, you got it, man, you got it." Then they rocked and rocked me as we drifted into sleep.

I opened my eyes to see Lionheart smiling at me. His teeth were sparkling diamonds. Percy snored on my other side. He was curled up like a baby and sucking his thumb. He cooed when I moved my body and stretched, then he started sucking even harder, maybe he was dreaming it was a hot cock in his mouth. Lionheart reached his elastic lips out to me and we kissed. The sky was growing brighter. It was a vibrant medium blue, but nowhere as bright as Lionheart's glowing turquoise eyes. He lifted his mouth from mine and waved with his hand toward the window. I knew this meant he wanted to go out on our patio.

Carefully, we disentangled ourselves from Percy so as not to wake him. Lionheart picked up the blanket from the foot of the bed. We climbed out on the fire escape. The breeze blowing off the river warmed my ass, which always gets cold when I sleep. It was Sunday morning; the docks were closed, the waterfront deserted. The sky to the east was growing rosy red. Across the river we could see the first pink rays of the sun reflected in amber tones off the tall spires of the new Twin Towers.

Lionheart quartered the blanket neatly and put it down on the fire escape. He sat cross-legged, facing the river, and held out his arms. I climbed into them, wrapped my legs around his hips, a position agreeable and familiar to me. His neck smelled like milk. I pressed my little tatas against his chest, and my nipples hardened like the pits of the pomegranate. Lionheart had a great forest of golden hair growing around the splendid equipment between his legs. I could feel some of these fine threads sticking in my already soaking, hungry snatch as I opened my legs wider. His cock was bent under me like a question mark. I pressed my whole cunt down on it, moving from side to side, tickling it with my labia, until I could feel it swell, stiffen, rise. I put my hands on his shoulders and lifted my body slightly, allowing his prick to spring straight up.

I lifted a little higher, a little higher, and it was in. Thick as it was, it slid smoothly right up into my belly. He grabbed my hips and moved me up and down, down and up on him. With every thrust his cock grew longer and longer, raising me higher and higher. Soon I was rising up, up above his neck, up above his head, up above the top of the window where I hovered, perched on his six-foot cock. I looked down at his beatific face. He smiled, blew me a kiss, and then his cock spread out inside me, growing, filling each and every cell with tingling bliss. I came like I had never come before, my whole self sparkling, dissolving into the glistening light. I knew I would be his forever; our bodies were singing together, making slippery, wet, musical sounds. Then suddenly I was on his lap again, his cock still rigid inside me, but returned to its usual erectile size. My tit was bobbing in front of his mouth, which had turned into a big red rose. This rose-petal mouth kissed my tit, then swallowed it whole. His tongue gobbling it, pulling it, pushing it way down inside me to tickle my clit. The pigeons perched on the roof just above us cooed softly as we moved faster and faster. Fiery sparks exploded up from between our legs. When he shot rivers of his jamboree juice up into me, I came once again, and the sun rolled happily up into the sky, turning the whole world gold.

He put his arms around my waist, pulling me close, and I could feel his heart beating. He was still so firm inside me. I wanted to sit on him until the end of time.

We were startled by sounds of applause and laughter. We looked down. A group of Japanese tourists were standing below looking up, taking pictures of us with their cameras. Obligingly, we smiled at them and waved, then I climbed off Lionheart. He stood; we bowed to our enchanted audience, and then went inside. Percy was still snoring. He was on his back now, still sucking his thumb, his hard-on poking up like a carrot.

Percy got a job as a stock boy at the Nature's Bower health food store on Atlantic Avenue. We had a great Christmas that year. Lionheart gave me thigh-high black leather boots. I gave him a red-white-and-blue-striped cock sock I got at the Come Again sex boutique so he could keep his dick warm when I was not around. We chipped in and gave Percy model trains, and he gave us vitamins.

Then our building was sold. The new landlords quickly discovered that I was the only one who had a lease to my apartment. Percy and Lionheart had sealed their deals with the old landlord with a handshake. They were given a month to leave.

A painter we knew had moved into one floor of a former spice warehouse a few blocks away on Jay Street. Lionheart went to talk to the landlord. The guy said that if Lionheart would fix it up, he would rent him a big, raw space that already had a kitchen and bathroom.

"It's a good deal," Lionheart said when he told me about it. "We'll have two homes instead of one. We can sleep there when we feel like it, and of course I'll be back here other times, keeping an eye on you." He reached over and pulled me to him by my long hair, just like a caveman. "That is, as long as you want me," he said, looking down, grinning at me, combing my hair with his fingers.

"I'll always want you," I said.

They fixed it up quickly. Percy had a nice, small room at the back. Lionheart put his studio in the front. He built a loft bed for us with a closet under it. I moved some of my best-loved books over there as well as an assortment of clothes, including half my lingerie collection and my favorite pink silk robe with the purple dragons on the back. Lionheart made a table out of wooden packing crates, then he set up his easel. He found an old, green brocade chaise longue on the street. He dragged it up for me to recline on when he wanted to paint me nude. Often when I finished posing, we would climb up into the loft bed, get under the covers, and suck and eat each other for hours. Lionheart loved chocolate. He liked to put M&M's in my pussy and eat them out while I held his sweet cock in my mouth and licked the tip like it was a lolly.

My family moved to Maryland because my dad changed jobs. My mother complained on the phone from their new home in Silver Springs. "It's taking me forever to unpack. Your brother is busy getting adjusted to a different school, and as you know, your father can't operate a roll of Scotch tape." She begged me to come down for a while and help her settle in. I took time off from work and went. Lionheart and I talked every day, but I still missed him.

I was going to return on a Sunday, but since I knew he had Saturdays off, I decided to come back Friday night. I would surprise him when he got home at the end of his shift. My mother, who thought Lionheart was my salvation, gave me a jar of homemade gefilte fish for him.

I got off the F train at the Jay Street stop at midnight. If I hurried, I'd get in before him. I wanted to be waiting for him dressed only in my black corset, legs spread wide, on the chaise longue. I remember how happy I felt when I reached the shelter of his building. I raced up the stairs, sure I had beat him in.

When I opened the door with my key, I did not find the empty room I expected. There was a candle burning on the table, and Lionheart was home. He was not alone. He was fucking a woman missionary style on the chaise longue. His big brawny rump was moving in and out, in and out, as he drove his cock, the cock he had promised would always be mine, back and forth into her like a pile driver. His mouth was buried in her neck. He appeared to be giving her a love bite, like he was always giving to me.

The woman's long silver nails were digging into his back. Her neck was arched, her great mop of black hair hung in corkscrew curls to the floor. I knew her. It was Tahini Schwartz, a dancer at the Whiskey.

It felt like an elephant had kicked me in the head. I stumbled forward into the room. "You bastard, bastard, you liar, you dirty shit!" I heard myself yelling. Lionheart looked up at me, stunned. Tahini looked up, too. She smiled. I turned, ran out the door, down into the street. I kept running all the way to my building as if the devil was following me. When I got to my place, I collapsed into my chair at the kitchen table and started to cry.

Tahini had appeared at the Whiskey in a cloud of patchouli. She was from Great Neck, Long Island, but liked to pretend she was some kind of exotic voodoo witch from Haiti or Brazil. She toted around a big red tooled leather pocketbook from Africa. She had once proudly displayed the contents of this bag to the dancers eating dinner at the staff table. She showed us stinky, smelly herbs that she'd sewn up in many little satin pouches; her douche bag, on which she had written *Sex Goddess* with a Magic Marker; and finally the dried head of a cobra she said was her spirit guide Boobaloo. I couldn't believe Lionheart's perfidy. The only explanation was that she must have bewitched him.

I felt empty and exhausted. I hadn't eaten since Maryland. There was no food in the house except for the jar of gefilte fish my mother had given me for Lionheart. I ate the fish straight from the jar and washed it down with a bottle of Boone's Farm Apple Wine that was in the refrigerator. Then I went into the bathroom and puked it all into the toilet.

The next morning Percy came over. He said he was dozing in his room when he heard me screaming. He told me Tahini had come over several times in the last few weeks. He'd been torn about whether to tell me, but then he thought it might just blow over.

"It didn't look like it was blowing over to me," I told him, and started to weep.

"You got it," he said ruefully, his pixie face red with embarrassment. "I didn't know what to do. I'm sorry; you know I love you." He picked up the bottom of his T-shirt, leaned over, and wiped the tears from my face.

"I just can't believe it," I said. "I thought he loved me."

"Me, too," he said. "I mean he's gone crazy; she's not even nice to him. She treats him really nasty, but he doesn't seem to notice. He looks at her like she's a Hershey's bar." This made me weep some more.

I couldn't bear the thought of seeing Lionheart and Tahini. I called in and told Eddie, my boss at the Whiskey, that I had caught ringworm on my butt at the Russian sauna and wouldn't be in for a few days. I took to my bed. Percy came to visit, bringing me a pound bag of M&M's. He told me Lionheart and Tahini had quit their jobs and that Tahini had moved in. He said she acted like the Queen of Sheba and was always bossing him around. Mandy Gerber, who danced as Catgirl at my job, called to see how I was and tell me that everyone missed me. I decided to go back to work. Shortly after that I bought a portable typewriter and started to write poems about my lonely life.

One day I decided to go to Lionheart's to get the stuff I left there. I knocked loudly at the door. When there was no answer, I used my old key. If Tahini had been a better witch, she would have changed the lock.

As I walked in, she came out of the toilet wearing my pink silk robe. Lionheart wasn't there. From where I stood, I could see into Percy's room. His things were gone. She must have banished him. Her eyes widened. I swear she hissed at me, sticking out a forked green tongue.

I made myself stand up straight. "I've come for my books and clothes," I said.

"I threw the books out," she answered. "Your other crap is in the closet."

I walked past her and opened the closet door. My things were piled on the floor. I picked them up and put them in my backpack. Then I surprised myself, affecting bravado I didn't feel: "I'd like my robe, please." She nodded toward the door with her head, indicating I should go, but I forced myself to stand my ground and keep staring at her. Finally she took my robe off and handed it to me, giving me a good chance to see her bewitching nakedness— her big high melon breasts, her black pubic thatch shaved into a swastika.

A month later, at work, I climbed down off the stage one night after my first set to see Percy seated at a back table. He was so happy to see me. He waved and jumped up and down in his seat, like a kid at a birthday party.

He told me how he woke up at four one morning to find Tahini seated naked on his chest. She was holding a straight razor right behind his ear. He could feel the cold steel edge sharp against his skin. "Either you go, or you van Gogh," she said.

"You got it," he said. He packed up and left that day. He moved into the Sunrise Hotel on the Bowery. The next day he got fired at the health food store. He was living by turning tricks under the West Side Highway. I gave him all my tips and told him to come stay with me, but he never arrived.

I heard that Lionheart had taken up photography. He was shooting head shots of Tahini and her friends. They set up a talent agency that failed.

At a McGovern for president rally, I met a soundman named Douglas. He had a mouth like Mick Jagger and a heart of gold. He gave me a black leather folder for my poems. He would go down on me for hours; still, too many times when we did it, I had to close my eyes and pretend he was Lionheart or else I couldn't come. I heard that Tahini and Lionheart were moving to Oregon, then I heard they were strung out on crystal meth. I heard they'd gotten hold of a VW bus and were making monthly trips to Mexico. Then I didn't hear anything about them anymore, and I didn't ask.

Howling in the Night

It was the summer that the women took off their bras in front of the big library on Forty-second Street and I was exploring what it was like to be a predator. I was tracking men, hunting them down for my own pleasure, experimenting with loving them and leaving them like the two-bit Romeos and Don Juans in the dime novels my mother used to read in the evenings when my father was down at Schenley's Bar.

I was the wolverine, the night hunter. I wore my long brown hair straight down my back. I painted my lipstick on red and thick as lust, then I would slip into a slinky minidress and go out on the prowl.

My favorite hunting ground was St. O'Doul's on Broadway and Bleecker. As soon as I got in the door, I'd scout the bar for a man who was hot. If I saw one and a seat next to him was empty, I'd head over, sit down, cross my legs, and let my dress ride up high on my thigh. I'd loudly order a tough, wild drink—a double green char-treuse neat or a triple shot of Cuervo Gold with lemon and salt—

then I'd ask him for a cigarette. If the seats next to him were occupied, I'd push right in and stand beside him.

I never brought anyone back to my place because he might want to stay over. I lied about my name, said it was Ruby, Rochelle, Rita, or Rosa. When I went home with a man, as soon as we were finished, I'd rise from the bed or couch or floor. I'd pull on my clothes.

He'd yell out, "Wait, I want your phone number," or "Hey, where are you going?" But by then I'd be opening the door.

"Ta-ta," or "Thanks, it was great," I'd call back over my shoulder.

Then I'd go to my apartment, take a shower, put a clean piece of paper in my typewriter, and write poems about Athena, Goddess of the Hunt, or Lilith the ur-woman, who came before Eve and had no shame. I had a job very suitable for a radical anarcho-feminist poet. I worked three nights a week as an exotic dancer at the Whiskey.

One night I decided to go to St. O'Doul's. I took a taxi across the Brooklyn Bridge into town. As I was getting out of the cab, the driver, who looked like Gurdjieff with an orange turban, said, "Beware of what you wish for, you might just get it."

A glance down the bar did not reveal any exciting prospects. There was a teddy boy from Wales, who had invited me home with him two weeks ago. He had a small red dick, and he jabbed me with it relentlessly as if it were a staple gun. I faked a fast big O and ran out of there. Now, he grinned widely and waved me over, but I gave him a quarter smile and just moved past him down the bar.

By the time I had settled on a seat, Fatso Louis the bartender was waiting for me. "How's the job at the Whiskey?" he asked. "How about if I choreograph your next dance?"

"I'm having too much fun being a baby doll," I said. "I don't need a new routine. If it's not broke, don't fix it. Since I'm off tonight, I thought I'd come down and watch you dance around the bar. I'll take a double Cuervo," I told him. I started to pull my wallet out of my purse.

"Put your money away," Louis said. "Tonight, Isadora Duncan, you drink for free."

I watched myself watching myself in the mirror over the bar. I saw the little girl deep inside who was so thrilled at all the manifestations of the experiential world that she couldn't sleep at night because she was afraid she'd miss something. I saw a pretty young woman with a hungry darkness around her eyes. The lights above the mirror fell on the bottles of booze stacked below, making the glass bottles sparkle with false promises of beauty everlasting and eternal life. The bar was filling up. An older guy with a mustache took the bar stool to my right. He ordered a Heineken and pulled out a racing form. His hands were grimy and covered with dust. I would not be asking him for a cigarette. I felt a breeze like a little swirl of wind, and someone slid onto the seat on the other side of me.

Suddenly the air around me had changed. It was sharper; it snapped and cracked with electricity. I smelled damp pine, mountain forests heavy with rain. My new neighbor was wearing wonderful cologne. I sipped my drink and forced myself to relax. I felt my ears concentrate on the sounds of his breathing. The excitement of the hunt made my mouth fill with saliva, my cunt lips moisten and swell. I pretended to be deep in thought as I counted from one hundred to one backward. Then, by lifting my head and turning it slightly to the right, I could take my first look at the prey sitting next to me. My neighbor was a wolf, a fine big strapping wolf with a salt-and-pepper pelt and large, elegant, black-tipped ears! He growled from deep within his throat, then he turned his magnificent head toward me and started to purr. He put his hairy paws out toward me in a gesture of entreaty. "Don't be frightened," he said. "I never bite beautiful women. I can be very gentle." Terrified, I turned my head away and fell back. Was I going crazy? My curiosity overcame my terror, and I took another look at my neighbor. I saw an older man with a long gray ponytail, wearing a black-and-white-checked shirt. He was not a wolf at all.

"Are you okay?" he asked. "You started to tremble and then you went real pale. I admit I was watching you in the mirror. Who could resist?" He gave me a friendly smile, and his perfect teeth gleamed white in his big handsome face. "I'm Frank Lupo," he said. I was still very shaky, but I managed to sputter out my name for the evening—Rosalie. I grabbed my drink and downed it in a gulp. "Here, let me get you another," Frank Lupo said. He caught Louis's eye and pointed to my drink.

"Thanks," I said, and took a better look at him. I noticed that the backs of his hands were covered with white hair, and the white hair grew out in big tufts above the collar of his shirt. What a virile beast! He was solid, husky. His arms bulged beneath his shirt, and his heavy thighs strained beneath his black chinos. He was a striking brute, my type any night.

When Louis brought my drink, I raised it in a toast. "To new friends," I said, throwing my cards on the table just like the big boys.

"I'm flattered," my new friend said. He told me he was from Wyoming; he was a filmmaker, documentaries. He was making a film about coyotes, and he was in town to do research at the Museum of Natural History. He rolled this out so glibly that I didn't believe him. He was either peddling magic mushrooms or dealing pot, I'd bet my panties on it. As I told him I was a writer moonlighting as an exotic dancer, it occurred to me that my story sounded as phony as his. Two drinks later, I wouldn't have cared if he was a mortician. He knew some funny jokes about the sex lives of animals. He moved closer to me and looked at me with such intense desire that I smelled my own animal scent wafting up. He leaned over me, stroking my hair and neck with his hot nose.

"Let's go back to my hotel room," he said. "I have some great still photos of Rocky Mountain bobcats I'd love to show you."

"Yes, yes, I just love bobcats," I said drunkenly. "They're my favorite cats; I like them even better than Siamese. They're very cute, yes, yes. . . ."

He put some bills on the bar for Louis. Then he put his hand on my neck and guided me out of the bar.

He was staying at the King Henry on Twenty-eighth Street and Park Avenue South. All the way over in the cab, he kept his big hot hand on the back of my neck, holding me as if I were a kitten. We said nothing as we took the elevator to his room on the third floor. He took his hand off my neck long enough to put the key in the lock. The back of my neck tingled, and I realized that he had been gripping me too tightly. I didn't want him to feel as if he was the one in control. We stepped inside. As soon as he locked the door behind us, I turned and, using all my weight, pushed him hard as I could back against the door. "What's this?" he said, surprised, but I didn't answer. Instead, with one swift motion I pulled down the zipper of his pants and yanked out his prick. It was already stiff. I inspected it like the joint of meat it was. It was uncut, surprisingly dark and veiny, gnarled, gray, thick and heavy in my hand. I didn't see any conspicuous sores, so I took him suddenly and roughly into my mouth and sucked him like I was a vacuum. I nicked him with my teeth; I showed him I could be nasty. I sucked him in deeper, rubbing the bottom of his cock up and down with my tongue, then I nicked him again. I bit him and held on until he let out a sound between a roar and a groan. Then I released him, stepped back quickly. He looked ridiculous with his pants sagging like a pair of panty hose around his ankles. His long purple rod pointed at me like an accusing finger.

Sneering, I said, "That's just a sample; you'll get more if you're a good boy." He had a furious look on his face but said nothing, just pulled up his trousers and zipped up the fly. At least he knows, I thought, that he's not with some silly little bimbo he can push around. He switched on the light and stepped into the room.

"I have something very good, if you'd like a drink," he said calmly, his voice not at all angry, but even and well modulated.

"Why not?" I said.

While he opened a large brown leather trunk at the foot of the bed, I looked around the room. It was the conventional hotel room, a big double bed flanked by matching night tables with matching lamps, two dressers with mirrors, a wide-screen TV. In the corner of the room there was a pile of fur pelts, black and glistening. "Thinking of making a coat?" I asked him.

"Perhaps," he answered. He had extracted a small cut-glass flask from the trunk and two standard shot glasses. His back was toward me as he bent to fill the glasses.

"What is that?" I asked. He turned to face me, holding a glass in each hand.

"From Wyoming," he answered. "The Indians make it; it's liquor made from prairie nutmeg."

"How quaint," I said, knowing he could not miss my mocking tone.

"To howling in the night," he said as he handed me my glass and then tapped it with his own. He downed his drink in a gulp, and I did the same. He put the glass down on the bed table, then he sat down on the bed.

Surprisingly, violently, he grabbed me by the wrist and pulled me down beside him. "So, you think you're a wild woman," he said. "I will show you what wild is." He kissed me so brutally his teeth cut right into my lip. I could taste the flat, metallic taste of my blood. His big tongue was pushing deep into my mouth, pushing way down my throat so I couldn't breathe. If he wants it rough, I'll give him rough, I thought, and I bit down on it. He pushed me away, snarling—his face twisted, feral, strained. "Whore, bitch, vixen," he yelled. Then he slapped me across the face so hard my neck snapped, then he slapped me again and again. My mouth was filled with blood; he must have knocked my teeth loose. This is nuts, he's a psycho, I thought. I have to get out of here. I struggled to rise but found I was so weak I couldn't lift myself off the bed. I had no strength in my back and hips. He ripped my dress off with nails so sharp they felt like claws. He bent over my breast and fastened his mouth over my nipple. He bit down so hard I screamed, then he sucked, and bit and sucked just as I had done to him when I had his cock in my mouth. It hurt terribly, yet I didn't want him to stop. Alternative waves of pain and pleasure washed over my body. He stopped and raised his head up. "So you think you're such a smart cunt," he said as his head moved down between my legs. He sucked my clit deep into his mouth. He used his teeth again. I thought he was going to chew it off. The waves of pleasure had ebbed away, and the pain was becoming more and more intense. I heard myself shrieking, "Stop, stop." I tried to pull back but could not move. I was in a vortex, spinning, spiraling down to a burning hell. He was looming above me again, his knees pressed sharply into my thighs, holding them apart. "Are you ready now, you pitiful bitch," he growled, "are you ready?"

He grabbed my arms and pinned them together above my head. From out of nowhere he conjured up a leather rope. He tied both my wrists together tightly, the stiff leather biting into my skin. My eyes shut in terror. I wanted to wake up and find that this was a bad dream, but when I opened my eyes again he was covered with thick silver and black fur. In place of his fine, long nose was an obscene hairy snout with a black tip. His fangs glistened yellow in his red mouth. His furry knees were already forcing my thighs wide, wider, until I felt I was going to snap like a wishbone. He dragged his razor claws down my body, cutting me, marking me with bloody stripes. I was being shredded, torn to pieces. Then he jammed his monster cock into me. It had grown three, four, five times in size. There seemed to be a sharp hook at the end of it, and with each vicious thrust he pulled my insides farther out. I screamed and screamed as it battered into me, but no one in the halls outside or in the adjacent rooms came to my rescue.

There was a great hot liquid feeling where we were joined, glued together with jism and blood. I was screaming and crying and hurting, but still I found myself arching up to meet him as if something in me wanted to come, to find some peace at the end of this pain. He was swelling, growing all around me into a terrible, menacing, giant furry creature, a Grendel, a monster. All I could hear was his panting, his rapid breath. He rammed inside me so roughly, I felt as if he had punctured the base of my spine as he exploded into me, discharging a flood of liquid fire. He collapsed on top of me, burying me. I fell back into the darkness.

Steel thumbs were pushing against my eyelids; my arms were stiff and aching. The leather cords cut into my wrists. I wanted to run away, but I couldn't move my legs—my ankles were bound, too. I was trussed like a chicken. I didn't know if it was day or night. I was alone in the same room to which I had come so boldly hours before. There was no trace of my brutal companion, except for a strong, bitter odor in the air, a combination of damp earth and decay. I wondered for a second if this was some kind of terrible LSD flashback, but then I looked down and saw that my whole torso was covered with long, deep scratches. Bloody scabs had formed around my nipples. I tried to move my wrists, to pull against the cord, and to my great surprise it fell open. He must have loosened it before he left. I untied the cord around my ankles.

There was a severe ache at the center of my body. Every part of me felt battered and torn. I think I slept. When I opened my eyes again, I was able to sit up, swing my legs over the side of the bed. I remembered his tearing my dress off, but now it was neatly folded on the chair, on top of my purse and shoes. I managed to dress myself. I checked inside my purse, relieved to find I had enough money for cab fare. The hall outside the room was deserted, and there was no one in the elevator I took to the lobby. The desk clerk didn't even glance at me as I rushed by, but an obese man in a red plaid sport jacket, sitting in a chair and reading a newspaper, whistled. "I'll give you twenty bucks, no, make that fifteen," he yelled.

Out in the street it was dusk. I had been in that room a whole day. The gods were finally merciful; there was a taxi right in front of the hotel. The driver said not a word to me as he drove through rush-hour traffic to my apartment.

As I paid him and climbed upstairs, I realized that I was supposed to be at work that night at eight. As soon as I got inside the door, I rushed to the phone and called my boss, Eddie, at the Whiskey. I told him I had the flu, a fever, I was throwing up, I had the runs. "Sure, sure," he said. "Isn't that what you had the last time? I need girls I can depend on. You called in sick three nights last month," he said. "I don't got no one to cover for you. You're fired, and don't come back here begging for a job when you get over these phony sicknesses." He slammed the receiver down.

I staggered from the phone and collapsed on my bed. I knew that what had just happened to me was real. My body bore the marks, but where had this terrible creature come from? Was he sent by an evil, vengeful male god to punish me for being a bad girl, for acting male, acting like a hunter? I went out last night so confident, and now I'm lying here wounded, jobless, covered with scabs. Maybe I created the monster out of some deep shame inside me. Had I been smoking too much chiba-chiba, reading too much Aleister Crowley? A little voice inside me said no. Maybe this whole episode was a kind of ordeal, a test of strength. Was I a true hunter? Did I possess the courage to keep prowling on the frontier edge of night where anything goes?

La Maison de Jou

I am riding the number 4 train uptown to the second day of my new job as phone girl at La Maison de Jou. It is a classy brothel with satin sheets on all the king-size waterbeds, and women who look like glamorous movie stars. Even the location is ultra-deluxe, a ritzy apartment building on East Eighty-sixth Street right off Central Park. La Maison de Jou occupies a former gynecologist's office on the ground floor, with a private entrance on the street.

Yesterday when he hired me, Ritchie Riviera, the owner, told me to call him Rocky or Big Rock, even though he is about five-feet, four inches tall and round and roly-poly like a kewpie doll. He told me that the mayor's brother lives in the penthouse on the eleventh floor and sometimes comes down for a little change of pace from his stuck-up society wife. He says the governor even stops by when he's in New York. He comes in wearing dark glasses and makes his appointments under the name of Joe B. Good.

It's a hot summer, even hotter than the summer of the Watts riots a few years ago. Still, I'm wearing an ankle-length maroon seersucker sack dress I got at the Salvation Army thrift store. I don't want the clients to confuse me with one of the working girls.

Even though I know prostitution is an ancient and sacred occupation, I don't want to have to make it with someone I'm not attracted to. My friend Judy Molloy from Provincetown is working in a place in the Haight in San Francisco. It's called the Zen Pleasure Dome. When we both lived in P-town, we would drive up and down the Cape in her old Ford Mustang. Often, when we saw an attractive hitchhiker, we would pick him up and invite him to come with us into the pinewoods. No one refused. Now she says it gives her great pleasure to have sex for money with men she doesn't know. She says it connects her to the life force of the cosmos. She writes me that I'd like it, but I don't want to; maybe I'm lacking in Zen. Perhaps, deep down, I feel it would be demeaning to sell the private part between my legs, yet I don't mind getting naked in front of men.

I had been working in a tiny G-string, dancing topless at the Whiskey and compiling my first collection of poems. Then a guy I picked up beat me badly. I was lucky no bones were broken, but I was left with long, deep scratches on my breasts, and black and blues over the rest of my body. I couldn't dance like that. When I called in sick, it was one time too many. My boss fired me. My friend Jilly had been working the phones at La Maison, but she got a lucky break, a part in *Hair*—lucky for her and lucky for me.

I look up, finished with my train of thought. The man across the aisle from me licks his lips, scratches his crotch. He is reading a *New York Post* with the headline "Ten Million Women Nationwide on the Pill." I wonder if this statistic includes the women at La Maison de Jou.

Yesterday, when he hired me, Rocky said, "The phones here are always ringing off the hook. Since Jilly left, I've been doing this job myself. I'm going crazy. I need someone I can depend on. You got an intellectual look with those big eyeglasses; you got a touch of class. You start right away, baptism by fire."

He took me into the living room with its purple velvet sofas and matching brocade drapes. He started to introduce me to the women he referred to as his "girls." "We got a real college girl," he said. "Eglantine here is putting herself through Barnard." He motioned toward a tall Lena Horne look-alike. She smiled, looked me up and down.

"We ought to call you Belle de Jour because of your blonde page-boy hair style," she said.

Then the phone started ringing. "You finish introducing yourselves," Rocky called out as he dashed out of the room.

"I'm Twiggy," said a delicate, tiny blonde, seated next to Eglantine. "We ought to call you Jackie O," she went on, "because of your big, round, brown-tinted eyeglasses."

"Yeah, you kind of look like Jackie O. You got her slim build," said a very busty woman seated on the other side of Twiggy. She told me her name was Anne Marie. She said she only hoped she could be as good a mother as Jackie O. She was raising her seven-year-old twin sons alone. Then Eglantine said Jackie O. had much better taste than Catherine Deneuve, and Anne Marie agreed. She looked like Anna Magnani except for that Jayne Mansfield bust. I didn't know how she could stand upright, but I was too polite to ask. The fourth woman, seated quietly in a tapestry-covered armchair, glanced up at me. "I'm called Georgia Peach. Hi, Jackie O.," she said in a small, wispy voice. Then she looked down again. She had blue eyes, freckles on her little nose, and flaming red hair. I could see through the transparent pink negligee she wore that she was a natural redhead.

Rocky came back into the room. "Come on," he said, "I'll give you the grand tour." First, he took me into the kitchen. "This is your office," he said. "We got two phones and this little switchboard." He pointed to the setup on the table, then he gave me a quick tutorial. I was to make appointments, answer the door, welcome the gentlemen, offer and mix cocktails. Before the clients went into one of the bedrooms with a lady, they stopped in his office to pay.

"No guy goes down the hall unless I see him first," he told me. He took me into a small room next to the office. Jammed into it were a desk, a huge color TV, two chairs, and a couch. When I asked him if he didn't find it crowded, he said, "An executive needs furniture." Then he showed me four well-appointed suites. Each suite had a mirrored ceiling, a bidet, a stall shower, and a toilet. The beds had satin sheets in different colors, red, blue, yellow, pink. There was a fifth room at the end of the hall that had black sheets on the bed. It was just like the others except that a big mirror covered one whole wall. Rocky then led me into the linen closet next door. Sheets, towels, and blankets were on shelves along one wall. The other wall was a two-way mirror; we could see directly into the room next door. "Of course, in that room, they can't see us," he said. "We get plenty of clients who just want to watch the action while they pull their bacon."

He led me back down the hallway past a tall mahogany cabinet. "That's the toy chest, where we keep the specialty items," he said. I was so busy thinking about the room with the two-way mirror that I didn't ask him what these specialty items were. As we entered the kitchen, the phone started to ring. "That's your cue, it's now or never, do or die," he said. I picked up the phone. Rocky coached me, "It won't hurt if you use a French accent," he whispered.

I had studied French in college. "Allo," I said, "you 'ave reached La Maison de Jou."

"Great," said Rocky, "you're a natural."

By seven o'clock all the ladies were booked for the rest of the evening. I answered the door and phones, smiled nicely, mixed drinks. At midnight when Rocky paid me, he gave me an extra twenty. "Take a taxi home," he said. "I like to treat my employees good."

Today when I ring the bell, Eglantine lets me in. "You're just in time," she says. "Rocky's mother brought over cream-filled éclairs. Where did you get that outfit? You look like a beet," she adds. She puts her arm in mine and leads me into the living room. I'm greeted by a chorus of "Hi, Jackie O."s. Georgia and Twiggy move over on the sofa to make a place for me. Twiggy takes a flaky éclair out of the white cardboard box on the coffee table and hands it to me. The sweet cream is laced with rum. I roll my eyes in delight. "See how she loves that sweet cream," says Anne Marie from the tapestry chair. "You could get plenty of that around here if you wanted." I try to smile as I shake my head. Rocky pokes his head in to say it is almost four.

I am on the phones until five, and then I start to let in clients. Most of the men belong to the Smith, Brown, or Jones families. They are well dressed in business suits or tailored slacks with snazzy sport shirts. At six-thirty I let in a skinny old man with a goatee. He has an appointment with Anne Marie in the name of Roger Brown. As I let him in, I glance at the pink Cadillac stretch limo standing at the fire hydrant outside on the street. The driver is eating a hot dog. "That's mine," the old man says. "I always keep it waiting."

Anne Marie seems to know Roger Brown very well. "Walter, oh Walter," she cries, rising from the couch and hugging him. Holding hands, they go into the Rock's office and then out again and all the way down the hall to the mirror room.

A few minutes later I'm making an appointment for a Tom Jones with Eglantine at ten. I glance up and see Anne Marie right outside the kitchen. She's opening the door of the toy cabinet completely nude, her breasts hang below her navel. Her dark brown nipples are big as dessert plates. She takes a peculiar flesh-colored apparatus that looks like a big Groucho Marx nose on a couple of strings. Then she runs back down the hall. I realize that the strange object is a strap-on dildo. The sight of Anne Marie's monster boobs has excited me, getting me hot and wet between my legs. I want to know how Anne Marie will use this contraption on Walter.

I can hear the sound of Rocky's radio; he's listening to the Yankees game. The others are busy with clients. Quick as a cat in the night, I steal down the hall and into the broom closet, carefully shutting the door behind me. A naked Walter is lying on his back on the bed. His hands are underneath his stringy rump, his legs jackknifed straight back over his body. He is very thin, but from where I am standing I can see between his sticklike legs. He has giant, fat pink balls almost as wide as his thighs. The hungry deep mouth of his anus gapes open, its edges red, puckered with need.

I watch Anne Marie kneel on the bed behind him. When she buckles the dildo on, she has a huge stiff prick rising out between her balloon breasts. With her hands she spreads Walter's ass cheeks apart. Her manicure is perfect. Her long crimson-taloned fingers stroke his butt cheeks gently. Then she draws her hips back and with one powerful thrust rams the dildo deep into Walter's ass. He twitches like a stuck frog and spreads his legs even wider. Now I can see his face. He is crying, but at the same time he is smiling, blissful, his eyes wide open, shining with tears. She starts fucking him harder, pulling her hips back farther each time, and then ramming in deeper. Every time she thrusts into his hole, her breasts bounce like gigantic beach balls. Her rampant flesh, his scrawny shanks remind me of Laurel and Hardy. In and out the mock cock goes. I wonder what it would feel like to have a big plug of rubber go in and out of my bottom hole. I want to put my fingers up there and pretend. I pull up my voluminous dress, but just then I hear the insistent sound of the phone. I dash out of the broom closet and run down the hall in time to get it on the fifth ring. I try to cool myself down with a soda from the refrigerator, but I can still feel that little hot spring bubbling between my legs.

Soon I hear Anne Marie's hearty laugh in the hall, then the front door slams shut. Walter is on his way. The door slams a couple more times, and I know that Georgia Peach and Twiggy have finished their sessions. I make several more appointments, and then the phone is quiet. I am filing my nails and reading *The Long Goodbye.* I'm at the place where Marlowe has just gone to bed with the sister of the woman his client was accused of killing. He is thinking that anyone with a bad conscience acts tough in bed, and then the doorbell rings. I glance at the appointment book. It is Georgia Peach's seven P.M., a man named Johnny Cordeira. When I look out the peephole, I see a wiry guy, medium height. He has light golden skin and a handsome face pitted with acne scars. He is wearing a big silver wedding band and a well-tailored khaki suit. He looks a little tired. I open the door.

"Good evening," I say. "You have an appointment? What time?" This is the way Rocky told me to check the guys out. This one doesn't say anything. He is looking at me intently, as if I am someone he knows from a former life. "What time is your appointment please?" I repeat, adding a sharp tone to my voice.

"Er, seven o'clock, Mr. Cordeira." He has a deep voice, an accent I can't place.

"Welcome to La Maison de Jou," I say automatically. "Come in." He is still staring at me. "Please come in," I say again. I open the door wider as he steps inside, then I shut it and lock it. He follows me into the living room. Twiggy is sucking on an orange lollypop and reading a Little Lulu comic book. Anne Marie and Georgia Peach are watching *Star Trek* on TV. They look up and smile their automatic, welcome smiles. "Mr. Cordeira is here, and this is our lovely Georgia Peach," I say, waving my arm in her direction. He is still looking at me.

"Nice to see you again, Georgia," he says to her, "but I hope it is all right if I change my mind." He turns to face me. "I want you," he says. I feel breathless, as if he had just put a hand under my skirt and pulled down my wet panties.

"No, no, no," I say, stammering. "I'm only the receptionist here. I make appointments. I don't have clients."

"I'll be your first then," he says. "I'll pay double, more if you like."

"Okay with me," Georgia says. "I haven't had a break today. Go ahead, Jackie O., you'll make more money."

Anne Marie chimes in, "We'll take care of the phones. Make hay when the sun shines, baby; go on, go in and tell Rocky."

Johnny Cordeira holds out a hand to me. "Please," he says, a plaintive note creeping into his voice, "you won't be sorry."

This is what I feared. If this guy looked like Walter, it would be easy to say no, but Johnny Cordeira turns me on. If I'd seen him at St. O'Doul's, I would have given him all my candy without his having to ask.

I hear the front door slam again, then Eglantine comes into the living room. "That Romeo went off like Sputnick," she says. "Now I can do my poly-sci reading for the next twenty minutes." Then she sees Johnny Cordeira. "Hi Johnny, am I the lucky girl?" she asks.

He starts to stutter, "Well, er . . . um . . ." Anne Marie cuts in. "No, Queen Bee, he wants Jackie O."

Eglantine turns to me, "Well, that's so nice, you'll have a great time, plus you can get more of those great dresses from the Salvation Army. Go ahead," she urges me, "we can take care of the phones."

"I'd rather not, Eglantine," I say, "thanks anyhow, everybody."

"Why not? What are you, a virgin, Miss Squeaky Clean? Do you think you're better than us?" Eglantine hisses.

"No, not at all," I manage to say. "It's just that it's not for me; it's not my thing, that's all."

"I'm sure you gave it away for nothing plenty of times," says Eglantine.

"No," I find myself repeating. "No, I just can't. . . ."

"Lay off her," says Anne Marie. "She's old-fashioned; she only does it for love."

"I am not old-fashioned," I say, my voice rising. "I'm, I'm . . . a feminist."

"Now that's old-fashioned," says Eglantine, "not shaving your legs, not wanting to wear sexy clothes."

Just then the phone rings, and I am saved. As I run down the hall, I hear Georgia Peach say softly, "Okay, honeybunch, come with me. I'll make you real happy."

The guy on the phone wants to know if Anne Marie is really a man. "Yes, she is, and Nixon is a Girl Scout," I tell him. I slam the receiver down. Eglantine has gotten to me. Do I think because I give it away for free, rather than make some useful cash, that I am a higher person? Am I afraid that if I sold my body, I would lose my intrinsic worth, that no one would ever love me, and marry me. But what about Judy Molloy? Her letters to me are so positive, so happy.

And what about intrinsic worth, isn't everyone holy? In Walter Winchell's column I read about the shady past of the spouse of a former governor. My four-times-married Aunt Millie once told me, "Whatever you do, don't let a man put that thing in you till you got a wedding ring on your finger. To a man, one hole is the same as another in the dark." I remember how sad I felt when she told me that and how I thought I never wanted to get married. After all, Betty Friedan says marriage is legalized prostitution.

Why have the forces of life got me to La Maison de Jou? Isn't everything in my life part of my karmic plan? My unique sea of love, as Ram Dass calls it. I know I am rationalizing because Johnny Cordeira is so hot; then I wonder what he and Georgia Peach are doing. I can hear the voices of the others arguing in the living room and Rocky's deeper voice joining in. "Remember, this is the La Maison de Jou—no bickering, no cat fights. Leave Jackie O. alone, Eglantine," he says.

Once again, I tiptoe down the hall and let myself into the linen closet. Again I silently close the door. Georgia Peach is beneath Johnny, he has one hand tangled in her hair and is kissing her. His other hand is beneath her, and from the way her body is elevated, it looks as if he has a finger, maybe two or three, right up inside her bum. He is moving his prick in and out of her, slowly raising his body so high that only the tip of his long cock stays inside; then with careful, slow deliberation, he sinks deep into her again. Georgia Peach is kissing him back, her limbs trembling. Her movements become more frenzied, as if she is starting to come, but he isn't going to let her, not yet; he moves even more slowly.

I wanted to be the one under him. This time my hand does make its way into my panties, and I put three of my fingers, all grouped together, inside myself. I start to move them in and out as he moves in and out of her. I pretend I am in one of those theaters on Forty-second Street where you go into a little booth and watch a couple do it on a stage, no danger of involvement, no danger of getting beaten up or falling in love. I imagine that I feel Johnny's mouth pressing hot on mine. Suddenly he breaks the kiss, lifts his head, his face flushed and wild. He looks directly at me as if he senses my presence, then he buries his mouth in Georgia's neck and starts to move faster. She raises her ivory legs and wraps them around his waist. With each strong thrust, he lifts her off the bed. I quicken the motion of my hand; it is me he's lifting, me he is moving, me he is carrying home. His eyes are shut and so are hers. I close mine and join them on this last stretch. I feel that familiar burst of heat burning away all the tension inside me. When I open my eyes, they are lying quietly, holding each other on the black sheets. I feel happy, light as air, as if I could do anything, go anywhere, to Majorca, Morocco, the Isle of Capri.

Instead I go back down the hall. When Johnny leaves a few minutes later, he makes a point of pausing and looking in at me in my office. He tries to catch my eye, but I won't look at him.

An hour before closing, two Asian men, Mr. Lee and Mr. Song Lee, show up. They've booked a double with Twiggy. They are wearing identical navy suits and look like twins except that Mr. Song Lee is totally bald. To my "Good evening and welcome," they just nod and mutter some unintelligible syllables. They are both strangely glassy-eyed. If they're too weird, Rocky will never let them go down the hall, I think. Twiggy stands up to greet them as I turn and go back to the office.

There are a few more calls after that, all for appointments the next day. Then I turn the phone off and get a Diet Coke out of the refrigerator. I put my feet up on the table and think about the cigarette of dynamite Mexican red that waits for me at home. I hear a faint, whimpering noise. At first, I think it is a mouse in the kitchen cabinet; then I listen more acutely. It is outside the room. I go out in the hall and follow the sound. Through the second shut door I hear a series of little, sharp cries. Something bad is going on. I run to get Rocky. He is dozing at his desk, the racing form spread out in front of him. "Wake up, wake up," I prod him, "there's trouble."

His eyes shoot open. "Where?" he asks. "Room two," I tell him. For someone of his bulk, he moves like a flash. He grabs the baseball bat from under his desk and runs down the hall with me a second behind him. He doesn't pause to knock; he just pushes open the door.

Twiggy is on the bed, her arms bound over her head with a leather belt. The bald Mr. Lee is kneeling between her spread legs. He is wearing a pair of shiny black cordovan loafers, black socks, and nothing else. His big prick is a strange gray color; it looks like a hairless rat. He is plunging it in and out of Twiggy's tiny slit. His companion kneels on the other side of him. All he is wearing is a pair of black leather gloves. He is holding Twiggy's thighs up, and his fingers are plunging in and out of her back hole. There is blood on the sheets and on her lower body.

Swinging the bat over his head and bellowing like Attila the Hun, Rocky charges. He hits the bald Lee on top of the head, and then he clobbers the other one even harder. The bodies of both men jerk and twitch like marionettes as they fall to the floor. Rocky hits each of them on the head again. Their eyes close as they black out, unconscious.

"You take care of her," he says, moving toward the door. "I gotta make a call. I'll be right back. If these animals move, you give a big yell."

Twiggy is sobbing and gasping for breath. I untie the belt. "We got you," I mutter. "You'll be all right." I try to gather her up in my arms, but she flings her head about wildly.

"How is she doing?" Rocky asks, coming back into the room.

"You can see," I say.

"Get a cloth and try to clean her," he tells me, replacing me at the top of the bed. "Don't worry, baby," he says in a soft voice to Twiggy, who is still sobbing. "You're safe now. We'll go to see the doc. He'll fix you right up. It's all my fault; I messed up bad. I'm so sorry, Twiggy. I must have fallen asleep, and they pushed you past me into the room. We took good care of those creeps; no one hurts my girls."

I start to leave the room to go fetch the cloth, but then the doorbell rings.

"It should be my friends," Rocky says. "Three big guys in suits. Just let them in."

When I look out the peephole, the men standing outside are as he described. The smallest one looks about six-five. They silently follow me down the hall.

"Get Twiggy's things and help me dress her," Rocky says. "These two are gonna get rid of these vermin. And this one, his name is Sinbad." He motions with his head toward the shortest guy. "He'll stay with you, settle up with everyone, and help you close the place. Don't say anything to the others. If anyone asks, just say Twiggy went home early. I don't want them to have a bad night. I'll talk to everyone tomorrow."

Within five minutes, the two terrible men have been hauled out the door into the night. Rocky has left, carrying Twiggy in his arms. Sinbad and I are seated across from each other at the kitchen table. We sit silently—it is almost midnight, and soon the last clients will be leaving. I listen to the faint traffic sounds outside. I imagine young couples, strolling hand in hand, walking home from a movie or a late dinner on this warm midsummer night. I want to be far away from the dark world behind the brocade curtains of La Maison de Jou.

"You're one cool customer," Sinbad suddenly says. "A lot of girls would have started bawling in there. Rock got lucky when he hired you." My insides are quivering like a bowl of jelly. It is hard for me to believe it doesn't show. My throat is so dry and constricted. I can't speak. Finally I manage to open my mouth. "How about a Diet Coke?" I say.

"Sure, why not?" he answers. The others all know Sinbad. After he settles up with them, he helps me straighten up, and then he takes me outside and hails a taxi. "You take care of yourself," he says as he opens the door.

The taxi driver drives down Seventy-second Street to Broadway, then heads downtown. We pass movie theaters and shops that are closed for the night, restaurants and bars that are open, still doing business. I feel sick. The jelly inside me has coagulated into a hard stone. I haven't eaten all day, except for that éclair. I close my eyes only to see Twiggy, thin and terribly pale on the bed, her legs marked with blood. I have the cabby let me off in front of the deli on my corner. The clock over the counter says two o'clock. It is already tomorrow. I buy an egg salad sandwich on rye and an early edition of the *Daily News*.

Upstairs, I fall into the only chair in front of the kitchen table. I devour the sandwich and glance at the paper. The headline says, "Jury Selection in Manson Trial Today." The footer says, " 'Let It Be'—Year's Bestselling Album." I am too agitated to flip the page and read further. I think about how bad Rocky must be feeling because he fell asleep. Working in a pleasure parlor is a risky business, but then there is no guarantee of safety anywhere. I remember the Mexican red in my stash box. After I smoke it, I feel calmer. I go into the bathroom and pull off my dress and my underclothes. On top of my daily hundred, Sinbad had slipped me an extra fifty bucks. "For being a stand-up guy," he said. I can manage for a while on a hundred and fifty dollars. I look at my body in the full-length mirror on the bathroom door. The purple welts on the top of my legs are fading to a blue yellow. The scabs on my breasts are peeling. I can start dancing again in a couple of weeks. Maybe I shouldn't even show up for work tomorrow. I notice for maybe the hundredth time that my right tit is bigger than my left. I wonder how Twiggy is; I wonder how badly she is hurt. She isn't a tough cookie; she isn't like Eglantine or Anne Marie. I think about the protective tone in the Rock's voice when he told Eglantine to lay off me, then I think about the toy cabinet and the mirrored room. I think of Johnny Cordeira. I think I don't want to go back to La Maison de Jou, but then, I just don't know.

Purple Panties

didn't ask his name; he didn't ask mine. He sat down next to me at the bar and ordered a gin and tonic, which is what I was drinking. After a while, he said, "I love the color of your hair."

My hair color is Clairol Sunrise Sunshine. I thanked him and said, "I like your hair, too." His hair was the color of carpenter's nails, and he had an old-fashioned Beatles cut, like Paul McCartney on the cover of *Rubber Soul*. He asked me to come home with him. I said yes. When we got there, he quickly, silently undressed and lay down on top of the sheets, his erection already halfway to heaven. Then I stripped down, except for my panties, my favorite purple panties.

He took my hand and put it on his cock. "My cock is hard," he said. I circled it with my hand and pumped it slowly five, six, ten times until it grew so big I could no longer close my fingers around it. "It's very hard now," I said. For an answer he pulled down my panties, my old, purple silk panties with the stretched-out elastic. I had them for five years at least. I could not bear to throw them out. When Lionheart gave them to me, he said, "My passion for you runs purple, red and blue, cold and hot." He is far, far away now, and this man doesn't know he is not the one I am thinking of as he pulls my panties down to my knees. He pulls them down so roughly that he scratches my thigh on one side, four angry, red lines. He pauses, takes a condom from a drawer beneath the bed, and slips it on. I am glad he has taken the initiative with this, so I start to kiss the latex tip, but he has no time for my tenderness.

He pushes me over on my side, my back to him. He runs his hand up and down my ass crack. "Smells like shit," he says. I say nothing as he pulls my shattered panties down my legs, pulls them off over my feet, and tosses them across the room. He tries to put his cock between my legs, but I don't move. He lifts one of my legs high with his hand and with the other hand he fingers my clit too hard, hurting me. I say, "Oww," so he stops and then he slides the tip of his cock up and down my slit, but I do not warm up quick. When he tries to push it into me, I'm still dry. "Touch my tits," I say, and he complies.

He takes each nipple between a forefinger and thumb and slowly pulls, elongating them until the heat rises in me and then he can slide in. He thrusts his cock deep, then he starts to move in and out rapidly, brutally, but I am wet now; I can take it.

I moan and groan and lift my butt up toward him. He puts his hand on my ass, trying to hold me still, but I want to move and I do. Then I put my hand between my legs and play with my clit until I make myself come. I smell blood and piss and then he spits out, "Douche bag, twat, bitch!" He doesn't like it that I have taken my own pleasure. He withdraws, rolls me over on my belly, and plants his knees firmly on my thighs. I could buck and throw him off, but instead I play submissive. I rest, let him think he is the master, and soon he finds his own rhythm. Again and again he slams himself into my pussy. I reach between my legs and play with myself some more. I force myself not to twist up and meet his insistent hips and I come again; I chew the inside of my cheek and he doesn't know. He starts to yell, "Whoo, whoo." Then he sticks his finger up my ass, draws it out, and shoves it under my nose. "Smell yourself," he says. "Do you like how you smell, you shitty cunt?" He tries to stick the finger that has little flecks of shit all over it into my mouth, but I close my mouth tightly, turn my head aside. He starts to ride me again, really riding me now. He is a pile driver, a ramrod. Then he comes like a dam opening up, pouring gallons of hot grease into me.

"Whoo, whoo," he yells again and then pulls out. We are on our backs but do not speak. We lie there like two quotation marks on top of the sheets. After a while, I get up, he has fallen asleep. I dress, leave. I get a block away when I realize I left my purple panties behind, but I don't go back, oh no.

The Beautiful Sadikka

A mysterious woman entered my life last month, and I did not invite her. Her name is Sadikka, and she gives my phone number out to strange men. She tells them she lives here. They leave imploring messages for her on my answering machine while I am at work, sometimes as many as four or five a day. "Please call me back, Sadikka," Oliver from Guyana says, while Gilroy pleads, "I'll give you anything you want, anything at all." Maybe she gives my number to the ones she is trying to discourage, or maybe she is a devil sent to pour salt in the moist crease between my legs. No men call me except for my father and my brother and my estranged husband wanting to know if he has gotten any mail.

The men who call for Saddika have names like Roland or Love-child, Jean François or Beaucoup Cool. They have island accents: They are from Haiti, Barbados, Trinidad, or Tobago. When I cannot sleep, I lay naked on my sheets, drink cheap rum and Diet Coke, and play back the tape on my answering machine. I finger myself and listen to the island men talk to Sadikka. I do not know the magic that makes a man's knees shake like the leaves of the banyan tree. I am not good at holding a man's attentions. I want to know Sadikka's secrets.

Sometimes they call when I am home, and I patiently explain that Sadikka does not live here, but they don't believe me, and as soon as I hang up, they call back again. Last week a persistent fellow named Ragout called three times, one right after the other. The last time he got so angry at me he started to yell, "Oh, Sadikka, stop talking in that squeaky white girl's voice. Why are you gaming me so?"

I imagine that Sadikka is black and very dark. I know she could be Asian, Indian, or from Kalamazoo, but I imagine her to be ebony, tall, coltish and saucy with an ass that sticks way out. She wears many silver bracelets, they go all the way up one of her arms, and she paints her fingernails and toenails Caribbean Blue. She has one tattoo, an island flower, a purple-and-orange hibiscus, growing across her midriff, curling up below her left breast.

She wears her hair in braids or cornrows, and her eyes are beautiful, liquid, filled with moonlight. I imagine meeting her: maybe in a thrift shop, where we are both looking through the leather jackets, or maybe at the health club, in the sauna. I will be trying to sweat out a hangover, my white body pale as a clam. She will come in and sit down next to me. I will know her by the music of her bracelets, by her tattoo. She will stretch her long frame out on the bench, close her eyes, and sink into the heat of the sauna. I will lie beside her and try to overcome my shyness. Soon her body will be glistening and covered with moisture, the hibiscus shining with dew. Finally I will speak. Although her beauty will make me stutter, I will compliment her on her tattoo. I will bring the conversation around to men, and when I ask Sadikka if she has a lot of boyfriends, she will say, "Why, honey, more than the days of the

week in which to see them!" When I ask her what her secret is, she
will throw back her beautiful head and laugh, her laugh like morning birdsong, and tell me something I already know. "Make them
sweat for it," she will say. "Don't be easy, don't be eager. Move slow
like molasses; keep them guessing. Show a lot of cleavage; wear per-
fume and sexy clothes."

"Oh, Sadikka," I'll say, "that does not come naturally to me. I
don't know how to play hard to get. Why should I play games anyway, and pretend to run away when I don't honestly feel like a tease
or a coquette? I want to be myself."

Sadikka will laugh again. "Because that is what turns men on,
sugar, they want to woo you," she will say. "Don't you know that?"

Sadikka is not a feminist. She believes her honeypot is her great-
est asset. She has one gentleman friend who pays her rent and
another who pays her health insurance. The butcher gives her
free steaks; the bus driver lets her ride for free. Before she leaves
the sauna, Sadikka tells me that I have a nice shape and that I
should make the most of it. I don't tell her I have a Ph.D. in self-
abnegation. Instead I say, "Yes, thank you, happy to meet you."
When Sadikka goes out the door, she leaves behind her the smells
of coconuts and papayas. I drink in her fragrance and think maybe
Sadikka is not a demon but an angel sent to guide me.

When I get home, I go through my clothes. I decide to give away
all the baggy grunge stuff that makes me look like a potato. I go to
the drugstore and buy Clairol Golden Sunrise Sunshine Blond and
dye my mousy brown hair gold. I clean my house and shave my
pubic hair into a heart shape. The next day I go to the Botanica on
Ludlow Street and buy a dozen of the pink candles that the juju
woman behind the counter says are for romance. I burn one whenever I am at home. When I walk on the street, I pretend I am

Sadikka: regal, coy, infinitely desirable. I get some wolf whistles; a man with one arm sitting in a doorway licks his lips, but this is not the gourmet I am hoping for. I don't go out to bars at night; I stay at home burning my pink candles. I eat only rice and bananas, hoping to loose five pounds and save some money. I don't even want to spend the two dollars it takes to rent a video because I am saving for a tattoo, an exotic flower like Sadikka's that will complete my transformation into a Calypso princess.

When I have enough money saved, I splurge on three rum punches at Raoul's and go to the Tarantula tattoo parlor on St. Mark's Place, where I choose an orchid to curl across my midsection beneath my breast. Despite the rum punches and the Novocaine spray Spider uses, it is quite painful, but I can bear it. I grit my teeth and imagine myself beneath a palm tree with an exotic island prince eating conch and oxtail stew.

When I get out on the street, I feel as open as the orchid on my skin, full of promise and ready to flower. My shirt covers my tattoo, but I can feel its power. A Rasta Romeo walks up beside me and says, "Hi, gorgeous." The next day when I get on the B25 bus, the bus driver waves my hand away from the coin box. "Beautiful mama," he says, "buy yourself an ice-cream cone."

My ex-husband calls about his mail. His tax return check has arrived, and he wants to rush right over and pick it up. I start to say sure, but then I surprise myself and hear myself saying in a new and lilting voice, "Oh, no, I'm busy right now. You can come later. Drop by in about three hours, say at ten o'clock."

"What's the big deal?" he wants to know. "You just have to hand my check to me."

"I'm busy," I say, "that's the deal. Come at ten o'clock or not at all."

"Okay," he says. "I'll be over at ten o'clock. I don't know what's gotten into you," he adds, then hangs up the phone.

I count my money and find out I have enough to buy some rum. I run to the liquor store and get it. I return, vacuum the house, clean the stinking cat litter, and light some jasmine incense. I take a long shower, let the hot water pelt down on me, and think how much I still yearn for him. I wonder if I have learned enough from Sadikka not to let it show. I rub my body all over with coconut oil, working it deep into my labia until they glisten. I take a long time choosing my costume and finally decide on some black, gauzy hip-hugging harem trousers and my black silk blouse. I wear no bra, and I knot the blouse tightly beneath my breasts so my orchid tattoo shows. I put out the lights and arrange the two pink candles in the candleholder on the table and light them.

When my ex-husband punches the downstairs bell at ten o'clock, I am ready for him. I let it ring five times before I buzz him in. When he is upstairs and outside my door, I do not answer until he has knocked several times. I open the door wide and just stand there so he can have a good, long look. Then I beckon him in, but he hesitates, gazing at me; finally he says, "God, you look so different."

"Come in, sit down," I tell him, but he remains in the doorway, gawking. I rub my hand back and forth across my chest until my nipples harden, and, using them to command him, I make him come in and sit down without having to speak a word. Moving as if in a trance, he sits in the rocking chair. Sadikka whispers in my ear, "Sugar, you are on the money now."

He manages to sputter out, "If you just give me my check, I can go."

I ignore him, move across the floor to the refrigerator, nice and slow, shaking my hips to a limbo beat. I am supple as a reed as I open the refrigerator; bending to get the rum and some juice from a low shelf, I wave my big, opulent bum at him. I make us drinks and bring them to the table, sit down opposite him, cross my legs, shimmy a little bit to the right so from where he's sitting he has to look at my tender cleavage, my puffy little navel.

"What's going on?" he wants to know, looking confused.

"Just relaxing," I say, smiling at him. I clink my glass against his. "Come on, drink up," I say.

"I just need my check," he says.

I decide to take a gamble, go for broke. "You need to kiss my sweet ass," I say.

To my delight he laughs.

Round one, I think, and Sadikka whispers in my ear, "There's your signal, girl. Move in for the kill."

"You know," I tell him, "I have been working hard on a story about spanking, but it's not going well. Without you around to help me do the research, I'm stuck." During our happier days he used to womp my rump with pleasing regularity. When I roll my eyes, he laughs again.

"You're so different," he says. "So relaxed."

"Thanks," I say, and ask him how his sculpture is going with only two months to his next show. He says he's feeling the pressure and starts to tell me about an idea he has for a six-foot-tall cross made of cigarette butts and condom packets. While he is talking, I notice his eyes keep straying to my tattoo, but I keep my eyes steady on his face and listen intently as if his words were divine revelation. He suddenly interrupts himself and blurts out, "When did you get that flower tattoo?"

"A little while ago," I say. "Do you like it?"

"Yes," he says. "Yes, I do."

"I'm so glad," I say, and give him a twenty-four karat smile. Suddenly, I hear Sadikka singing, "Day-oo, day—ay—ay-ooo. Daylight comes and I wanna go home." My husband puts his big hand over mine.

"I've been thinking about you a lot lately," he says, his speech slurred from the rum.

"What about me?" I say.

"About the good times." He tightens his hand over mine. "But I'd forgotten how beautiful you are." He leans forward as if to kiss me, and just then the phone rings. I don't want to interrupt this extraordinary moment so I say, "I'll let the machine get it."

My ex moves closer to me as my voice chants out my phone number and the machine beeps; then a deep male voice comes spilling out into the room.

"Hello, you sweet, sweet thing," the voice says. "This is Fontaine. I want to see you again as soon as you are free. I want to smell that pretty flower you have on your chest. Call me," he says, and then he makes a series of loud kissing sounds. The room is totally still. I can no longer hear Sadikka in the background.

"No," my husband says, shaking his head, pulling back from me, and standing up. "Uh, uh, uh," he stammers, and then he turns and runs out the door. I can hear his steps thudding away down the hall like a hammer pounding nails into my coffin. All my island glamour vanishes, and I feel myself dissolving into a puddle of tears. I want to run after him, beg him to come back. I can hear how I would plead, "It wasn't me Fontaine was yearning for, it was Sadikka." But he probably wouldn't believe me anyway.

"Saddika!" he would say, "What is this crap about a Sadikka?"

I get the rum and start to guzzle it straight from the bottle. With any luck I should be able to drink myself into oblivion within a half hour. *See what happens when you try to make yourself over?* I think. *You're a lost cause, a pathetic bookworm trying to be a glamour girl. You're a flop, a fool, a phony.* Suddenly I hear footsteps running in the hall again and then a pounding on my door. *The men in the white coats are here at last,* I think.

"Who is it?" I cry out, getting up to make sure the door is locked. But then a familiar voice says, "Please, it's me, let me in."

I open the door to see my husband standing there looking all hangdog and sad.

I want to say, "Listen, that guy wasn't really phoning for me." But I am boozed up and can't speak, my tongue drowned in rum.

Finally he blurts out, "Are you serious about that guy?"

"No," I say, then add, "but he wasn't really calling for me."

My husband isn't listening. He's smiling and looks relieved. "Can I come in?" he says.

I open the door, and he strides inside. "I can't blame you for getting lonely," he says. "I've been feeling lonely myself. What are you supposed to do, camp out by the phone waiting for me to call?"

This is miraculous, wonderful, fantastic. I hear Sadikka's bracelets jingling like little laughing bells; I feel her strong supple hands on my back, and she pushes me right into his lap.

Somehow our lips join as rightly as they did when we first kissed. My husband's big arms wrap around my back. Sadikka is singing "Day-oo," and after a time I put my tongue in my husband's mouth and he sucks it slowly, savoring it like guava butter. Then we pull away from each other and start dancing with our eyes. I can't stop my tongue from darting out and tracing the line of his lips. I hear myself say with a soft island lisp, "Well, maybe I have been such a bad girl that I deserve a spanking." His eyes light up, and he gives me a big come-on smile. I stand up and peel my hip huggers off; I do a slow pirouette, showing off my white lace bikini panties and fat pink behind. I slowly slide my panties off and down my legs and toss them on the table next to his drink. Then I turn around and shake my behind at him. It doesn't take long for his manly nature to rise in all its ten-inch glory. I lie down over his lap and offer my bottom up to him like a flower. The delicious heat of his big hard cock warms my belly. The first whack of his hard palm on my bottom is a shock. "Was that too hard?" he asks.

"Oh, no," I reassure him. "Please husband, punish me."

He continues to paddle me. Each smack of his hand heats the springs bubbling between my legs. Soon my bottom is steaming, and I think I'm going to burst into flame. When he stops flailing me, he puts his hands beneath my arms and lifts me up in front of him. My dark bush is above his mouth; he puts his wily tongue into my slit and teases me slowly. My love dew bathes his face, and he sniffs appreciatively. I feel the beginnings of the short, intense convulsions inside me that mean I am about to come, but he raises his face. He says, surprising me, "I love you." Then he gets up and lies backside down on the kitchen floor so I can ride him. His sex is as swollen as a ripe mango. As I settle in, I hear Sadikka crow, "Take it slow, girl; take it slow."

Sweet as Sugar Candy Cunt

The stuntman pulled his head out from between my legs and sat up among the tangled sheets, his mouth and chin wet and slick with my love oils. He looked annoyed, his face all twisted. He had a little belly that I liked to rub, but now it quivered as he breathed hard, my angry Buddha. I put my hand out to rest on his knee. I always wanted to touch him. His face relaxed, and he patted my hand, grinned ruefully, then reached into his mouth and pulled something out. He showed it to me on the tip of his forefinger. It was a stiff, black whisker.

"Oh," I said, "you have a souvenir, one of my cunt hairs."

"Right you are, you win the prize," he said, no longer grinning. "You didn't do a good job shaving. And," he continued, his voice rising, his tone sharp, cutting like a whip, "don't use that word. I hate that word, it's ugly." I was shocked. I loved the cunt word, the ripeness of it, the guttural, dark sweetness. It was like a ripe, purple plum. It made me think of fat, swollen pussies, of Constance Chatterley and Mellors, of pulling my panties down in a dark, dirty alley off a waterfront street and opening myself to a skinny punk with a dagger tattooed on his arm. Besides, I loved all the so-called dirty words, fuck and prick and cock and pussy, too.

"I love that word," I told him. "It turns me on; I love all those words."

"Well, you better not say it in front of me; just don't use that word in front of me," he yelled. His lower lip was trembling like he was a little boy about to cry.

"What do you want me to call it then?" I asked. "Twat, coochie, honeypot, joybox, snapper?" He was wiping his face dry with the palm of his hand. "Or how about slit or monkey, or the old English quim or quiver? You're always saying you love Shakespeare; are those words somehow cleaner than cunt, better than cunt?"

"You're really beginning to bug me," he shouted, and he got out of bed and went into the kitchen. Through the open bedroom door I saw him take a cigarette from his pack on the table and angrily light it.

This man, who did not like the word *cunt*, approached me at an art opening and told me that I was beautiful, that I looked like Gypsy Rose Lee. He had a face like Russell Crowe in *Gladiator*, a wide meaty back, and big solid haunches. I thought I could ride him a long, long way—maybe to Russia. I would ride him through the streets of Moscow in the snow; the heat rising from his strong spine would keep me warm.

Over our dinner, I found out he was a stuntman who read Hunter Thompson, Bukowski, and Mavis Gallant. His favorite actor, Clint Eastwood, is my favorite actor. Later, in my bed, I found out he could be rough, just the way I like it. He tied my wrists behind me with my pretty red bra, pulled my thighs apart with his big, rough hands, and shoved himself inside me with the strength of ten demons. I screamed, but then he just pushed harder. Then he started to move very slow; the wetter I got, the slicker I got, the slower he moved. Demon! He knew just what to do. He gathered both my nipples in his mouth and bit down hard; the intense pain yielded to ecstasy. He started ramming me with great force, hammering, pounding into me until the ceiling of heaven opened around me and I saw God. I came so violently the room shook, and then I saw shooting stars, meteor showers, a night sky scorched by flame. He pulled out and shot across my chest. I know that when I get religious while I'm having sex, I'm in big trouble, but at least I managed not to say "I love you" by biting down on my tongue. It was the best fuck I'd had since the day Ronald Reagan got shot, when Lionheart and I got excited watching the TV coverage and started screwing on my old red velvet loveseat.

On that first night, the man who didn't like the word *cunt* rubbed his come into my breasts with his still hard cock, then he pointed to the thick, wiry growth between my legs. My ex-husband used to call it my passion pelt, my nirvana bush, sometimes—the ultimate pussy deluxe; but this man, whose name was Buck, said, "Shave that off."

"Don't you like it?" I wanted to know.

"Shave it," he answered. "It's nicer." I was still so in awe of his fuck power that I didn't even ask him why. I shaved it the very next day. It took me an hour, and I managed to cut the inside of my leg, a tiny crescent-shaped cut that looked like the waning moon.

Buck sat in the white wicker rocker in the kitchen, smoking his cigarette. I pulled the sheets over my head like a child playing hide-and-seek. Under the tent of the sheets I thought it smelled like the Garden of Eden, like sperm and snake oil, crusty pussy and sweat. I didn't want to be mad at him. I poked my head out. "Let's go for coffee and bagels at Taj Mahal Bagel," I called. "My treat."

"You got a deal," he said.

Later that day, after he had left, but not before kissing me and branding me with three diamond-shaped hickeys on the top of my breast, I couldn't stop thinking about him. He doesn't like hairy pussies; he doesn't like the word *cunt;* he seems to love my Tinkerbell tits, my Peter Pan frame. Maybe he wants a little Lolita; but then I want a big bruiser, sometimes even a nasty Marine. If he's objectifying me, I'm objectifying him, too, but how could he not love the word *cunt,* with that soft, groaning *u,* that wonderful *u* sound that is in *udder* and *mother.* Even Clint Eastwood uses the C word, but then Clint doesn't say *cunt* exactly; *cunny* is the word he says in one of the first movies of his I saw. But cunt or cunny—I still think it's a beautiful name for a beautiful part of me.

The next time the man who didn't like the word *cunt* came over, he took me for a nice dinner at Angelino's. Over the scungilli and red sauce, it was difficult for me to resist the urge to raise my glass of Chianti and toast: Love me, love my cunt. After the espresso and cannoli, even after the anisette, I was still upset with him.

Later that night, back in my apartment, when I was naked on all fours and kneeling at the edge of my bed, he put his hands on either side of my ass and held me so I couldn't move. He stabbed his cock in and out, impaling me fiercely. I wanted to pull my cunt away from him and ask him to say, make him say, I love your cunt, your juicy cunt, your sweet-as-sugar-candy cunt, but I did nothing, said nothing.

Then, afterward, I couldn't fall asleep. I watched him sleep on his back, his mouth open. He snored slightly, a happy hum like an air conditioner. His head was large like the rest of him, but he had small, shell-shaped, delicate ears. Suddenly I leaned over and whispered into a pretty pink ear, "Cunt, cunt, cunt, cunt, sweet-as-sugar-candy cunt. *Cunt* is a beautiful word, cunts make the universe, cunt, cunt, cunt, cunt." He stirred in his sleep, shook his head from side to side vigorously, no, no, no, as if he had heard me.

"Cunt, cunt, cunt," I whispered in his ear again, and then, "Cunny, cunny, beautiful cunny." He shook his head some more, began to thrash about, but I showed no mercy. I chanted into his ear until I started to feel silly and got tired of it, then I curled up beside him and drifted off.

When I woke the next morning, he was already awake, sitting cross-legged beside me. He had big, dark circles under his eyes and was puffing away furiously at a cigarette.

"Hi," I said, "how did you sleep?"

"Lousy," he answered. "I had the weirdest dreams."

"What did you dream?" I asked him.

He colored slightly. "Oh, I don't know," he said, "weird stuff."

"Did you dream you were wandering in a dark, twisted cave with hairy walls, or that you were lost in a forest at night and you couldn't see anything at all but you could smell the wet moss, the compost smell of growing things?"

"Yeah," he said, "something like that, how'd you know?" He had a puzzled look on his face.

"Maybe you ought to talk to Dr. Freud about your dreams," I said.

"I'm not in the mood to be analyzed," he shot back. "I'm going to take a shower." As he moved across the floor toward the bathroom, I couldn't help notice that his chunky bottom had grown larger; it sagged like an old sofa cushion.

I heard the sound of the squeaky faucet turning, and then the sound the water made as it struck the plastic shower curtain. "Why is the shower so filthy?" he yelled. "Don't you ever clean it?"

"Shove it up your lard ass," I called back.

"What, what did you say?" he bellowed.

"Clean it yourself," I yelled. . . . There was silence.

In the silence I saw in front of me the dingy, gray underbelly of love. In spite of the powerful currents running between us, we were not on the same frequency. But maybe I was making too much of it; after all, *cunt* is one of those expressions, like *Al Sharpton* or *enema*, that people have strong reactions to. So what if Buck didn't like the word *cunt* as long as he liked me? But he didn't seem to like me much right then.

A few minutes later Buck emerged from the shower with my strawberry pink bath towel wrapped about his waist. He really looked hot, and seeing him, I couldn't feel as angry as I had just a few minutes before. But what did I feel? I didn't know exactly. I had to figure it out.

"You look so sexy in that skirt," I said, making a joke the way I often do when I'm blocked or confused or feeling pain. But he didn't think it was funny.

"I don't need your comments," he barked. "I gotta get out of here." He dressed in a flash and headed out without giving me so much as a peck on the cheek. As he was opening the door, he turned and mumbled, "I'll call you."

I smiled back at him, "Cunt, cunt, cunt," I said. He slammed the door behind him as he fled.

The Motion of the Ocean

One night I had a dream that Ron Jeremy, the gnomish porn star from Queens, was in bed with me; he was naked but he didn't want to screw, he wanted to talk about our teaching careers. He used to be a special education teacher, and I teach sex writing. "We have so much in common," he said, "there's nothing more special than teaching people about sex."

"Unless it's having sex," I countered. He sagely nodded his head as he stroked his famous tool.

I dreamed about him because I had just read an interview with him in *Time Out New York*. He claimed that despite his nine-and-a-half-inch penis, women constantly tell him that it is not the size of the boat but the motion of the ocean. I flashed back to that postcoital feeling, so akin to drifting in the gentle fluids of the womb, my whole being all too briefly afloat in a warm cosmic sea of hope. I used to get that motion of the ocean feeling after sex with three-inch Sam.

I am being vindictive here, it was actually four inches erect. The first time we talked at my local bar, the Right Bank, his deep, hoarse, sandpaper voice made me instantly wet. He sounded like a tough guy, a gangster in the old movies. He told me it was because he used to be a chain smoker. When I said he could chain me up anytime, he smiled and asked me for my number. He even looked like a gangster, an enforcer—big, dark, and burly. Since he was such a husky guy, the three inches was something of a surprise, but I couldn't have cared less. I loved doing it with him even if his cock was not much bigger than the middle finger of my right hand. I would have chosen him over Ron Jeremy any day. He had a way of fingering between my bum, while he sucked my nipple, that drove me wild. Besides, he was a smart guy, a journalist, and a big reader. We would talk about books for hours. I loved how genuinely interested he seemed in what I had to say. After the old in-and-out, he liked to make a hammock of his arms and rock me as we talked.

One night, after we had been together six months, the postcoital conversation took a shocking turn. I thought I had just given him the rimming of his lifetime. I was talking about our studying Tantric yoga together when he interrupted me. "I have to break this off with you," he said. "I want to see other people, and I know you believe in monogamy."

The very first night we were together, I'd told him how I'm not good at sharing. "I become jealous, crazy, competitive, I refuse to believe that *the other woman's* pussy could be as fine as mine," I confided. "I cannot control these evil, base thoughts, and I hate myself for thinking them, so I just refuse to be in that kind of situation."

He had replied, "I'm all for one at a time, too."

"What changed your mind, or were you lying?" I found myself yelling at him.

"I'm really sorry," he said. Silently, quickly, he dressed and left, ignoring my crying. Later, I wondered if he was using my position on monogamy as an easy out; then I wondered why I just couldn't accept that he was a louse. Now when I see him at the bar I say hi but sit far away from him. Sometimes I glance up and catch him looking at me, and then I feel like sticking my tongue out and yelling, Fool, coward, loser, but instead I turn my head away and suck vigorously at my straw, even if my glass is empty.

I manage to throw off the lead weights that have been holding down my body, and I swing myself out of bed. The alarm clock on the bed table says ten-thirty, and I had set it for seven. I have slept through my writing time, my magic words dissolved in last night's four vodka and tonics. My foot hits the *Time Out New York* on the floor. I remember Ron Jeremy said that he always tells the girls, "Don't look at me as a porn actor, look at me as still being a teacher." I wonder if my students are half as eager to see me as they would be to see Ron Jeremy strut his stuff. I don't feel very much like a teacher as I totter to the bathroom. The room tilts at a 45-degree angle, and I am afraid that I am going to slide down through the floor, but I manage to make it to the relative safety of the commode.

My butt cheeks rest in the comfortable groove I've worn in the old pine toilet seat over the past twenty years. I tell myself that looking away from Sam at the bar is an accomplishment; there was a time when I would have given him another chance to hurt me. I tell myself that not jumping into the East River is an accomplishment, but I still feel futile and sad. I try to recall my plans for the day: writing, correcting student papers; then I was going to do the laundry, and why . . . Today is Friday. Murphy's sex party is tonight.

Murphy and I met outside City Hall at a demonstration protesting the closing of the AIDS clinics in East New York. He was standing next to me. His poster said: IT COULD BE YOUR SON. The one I had made said: IT'S HUMAN RIGHTS, NOT GAY RIGHTS. He told me he was a tap dancer and a performance artist. I told him I was a sex writer and a teacher. He asked me if I had a girlfriend. I answered that I like girls once in a while, but I really spread for men. He said he felt exactly the same way and invited me for a margarita. Since then we have shared many margaritas and a couple of men.

A while ago he phoned me up and said he wanted to have a sex party. He had read about a Viagra party in a loft in Dumbo in a *Village Voice* article. "How are you going to get the Viagra?" I asked him. "Rob Bob Dole's medicine cabinet?"

"Who wants to throw a copy-cat party? Stuff the Viagra," he said. "I want to create a sexy party without Viagra, but with performances, music, wonderful food, places for public intimacy and private fun. My roommates think it's a great idea. We'll charge a five-dollar cover for expenses."

Murphy lived in a big loft on top of an old pretzel factory in Red Hook with the four other members of his radical performance group, Campfire Girls. "Of course, it's pan-sexual, like all our other events, but as usual we'll probably get more gays and bi's than straight people. Anyhow, you have to come; I need your radiant presence."

"Whoa," I said. "Whoa. I don't want to be there. Orgies turn me off. Didn't I ever tell you that? Didn't I ever tell you about the Sexual Freedom League party I went to up in the Berkeley hills during the summer of so-called love? The sight of all that furious, naked random sex got me upset. It seemed so ruthless. I heard a man tell his wife, 'You got yours last week, now bug off while I get mine.' I wanted to leave, but my clothes were under a bed on which a bunch of people were fucking. I spent the rest of the party outside the house, naked and puking under a eucalyptus tree. At two A.M., when the party broke up, I went back inside and got my stuff. No more orgies for me!"

"It's not 1968 anymore; this is the twenty-first century. We are more sophisticated about sex. We have more couth," said Murphy.

"That's questionable, Murph. I don't think I want to go."

"You always enjoy yourself at our events," he said, "and I need you and your shy tits there; your beauty enhances the room. Also, Miss Sour Pussy, don't think I don't know how since Sam dumped you, you spend your nights hanging out at home. I bet you watch John Carpenter movies and play around with your navel-piercing, trying to make it bleed. You're turning into a hermit. Come on, come to the party; it starts at nine." I knew that Murphy was right and that I was lucky to have such a good friend. "All right," I told him. "I'll wear my white latex sheath dress."

"That's my girl," he said.

Murphy's street in a run-down semi-industrial neighborhood was usually deserted at night, but this evening cars were parked all up and down his block. The white latex dress stopped high on my thighs, and a balmy summer breeze played between my legs like a teasing finger. I felt like I was on a movie set. I was the hooker with a heart of gold or the dance hall girl, a single mom coming home after a long, long night.

I walked up the stairs, rang the buzzer, and heard the click of the peephole being opened. I knew I was being inspected, and then the door swung open. A huge woman wearing a white sailor suit with gold buttons was standing before me, smiling. Her breasts, under the suit jacket, were the size of beach balls. She had long, thick red hair down her back, like the mane of a horse, and perched precariously on her head was a rhinestone tiara. She was grinning at me as if we were old, old friends.

"Ensign Penguin at your service, pretty lady," she said in a deep voice. She was a man. "May I have the honor of making your acquaintance?"

"I'm Murphy's friend Colette," I said.

"Oh yes, I thought so, you're expected," she said. "Complimentary admission; he told me to give you a big welcome." Ensign Penguin leaned down and kissed me wetly on the cheek. "I love your frock, so very tarty," she said. She took my hand and led me inside.

The large, high-ceilinged room was lit by blue light. Clusters of pink helium-filled balloons floated up by the ceiling, giving the room a festive sweet-sixteen-party air. The loft was filled with people moving through the dimly lit room like figures in a dream. The voice of Peggy Lee was singing, "Fever, fever all through the night. . . ." In the big open kitchen, the banquet table was piled with food. At the very back of the room, a low stage had been built.

"Here," said Ensign Penguin, pressing a paper into my hand. "Read this, and have a wonderful time." Then she winked at me and turned back toward the door. In the blue light I couldn't make out what was printed on the paper, so I moved into the kitchen to look at it in the light from the candles burning on the table. "WELCOME TO THE LUSTY LOFT!" it said in black italic script on a fluorescent orange page.

"Guidelines: There's a lot of space here—explore it! And claim it, too! Please respect the STOP signs. There are dams, lubes, condoms, or wipes throughout the space. We encourage you to use them.

"Problem solvers are wearing tiaras. Find them if you have questions or need help. The front kitchen is cool-down space, home base for problem solvers, refreshments, snacks.

"Take responsibility for your own actions regarding substance use. Consider using in moderation; not everyone wants to be hit on by someone who's fucked up.

"We are all free and different people. It takes a conscious effort by all to create a safe environment. Please respect others' boundaries.

"This is a kink-positive space.

"ENJOY!"

Only Murphy could have written this, I thought; he covered all the bases.

"Colette, Colette, you look just like a movie star in that dress, you look like Marilyn Monroe in *Niagara*," someone yelled. I turned to see a man coming toward me wearing nothing but a long grass skirt, and a tiara atop his short brown hair. It was Gino, one of Murphy's roommates.

"Thanks," I said. "You look like a movie star, too. You look like Dorothy Lamour in *The Road to Bali*."

"Well, thank you so much," Gino said.

"You've done a great job," I told him. "Where's Murphy?"

Gino motioned toward the back of the room with his hand. "I last saw him by the stage," he said. "I'll show you around, and then we'll go find him."

"Let me get a drink first," I said. I poured myself a glass of white wine, and immediately downed it. It would help me get over the shyness I was feeling. I helped myself to a stuffed grape leaf from the food table. There was a big bowl of condoms next to the potato salad.

"We made those stuffed grape leaves yesterday," Gino said, "and you must try the red pepper spread. Do you like my tiara? It was Mickey's idea that the problem solvers wear these." Mickey was Gino's long-time partner.

"You look so hot, I want to check out what's under that grass skirt myself," I said. He laughed and took my hand as he guided me into the room. Directly in front of us a naked man and woman were seated, embracing tenderly in a big blue plastic kiddy wading pool that was filled with water.

"Water sports?" I asked.

"You win the brass ring," was Gino's answer. "Come, see what we've done with our rooms." He led me across the floor; partitions had been built to create four small rooms, along the wall.

Gino led me into the room I knew he shared with Mickey. "See," he said, "we put all our personal stuff in the closet, and then we tacked up that red curtain and pinned the DANGER sign on it. Murphy negotiated a deal on a bunch of air mattresses at the sporting goods store. We put one on each side of our bed. Everyone else did pretty much the same. Look," he motioned to a small end table with a tray full of condoms, a big tube of K-Y, and large bottles of Astroglide and Liquid Silk. "We put one in every room. We put our nicest linens on our beds and on the air mattresses. Then we got these blue bulbs and put them in the ceiling fixtures."

"It looks like a harem or a seraglio," I said.

"Yes, that's the idea," said Gino, "*Arabian Nights* meets *Boogie Nights.*"

Back in the main room it was even more crowded. Peggy was singing, "Everybody's got the fever," as people danced in couples or groups of three or four. Under the blue lights the scene looked like an enchanted cotillion or a Beaux Arts ball. The odors of sandalwood, patchouli, and vanilla floated in the air. I craned my head, started to look around for Murphy.

Just then a heavyset woman with short, black, spiky hair ran up to Gino. She was wearing a red sarong that started just below her pendulous breasts. "There's no toilet paper left in the loo," she said to him in a British accent.

"I'll take care of it," he said. "I have to do this," he said to me. "See you later, gorgeous."

As he turned away, I got a look at the woman's face—it's Sophie, sweet Sophie from Liverpool. We met at the Nyorican Poets Café. She was part of the British slam team. We spent a sizzling night together. "Sophie, Sophie," I called to her. She swiveled around and saw me, and her lovely face lit up.

"Oh, Colette, it's you," she cried out. "I was wondering how to go about finding you." After our love feast in her hotel room, she was in such a rush to catch her plane, and I was so late for work, that we separated without exchanging addresses.

"What are you doing here; how did you find this party?" I asked.

"I'm in Murphy's tae kwan do class," she said. "I moved here, you know. I got a job teaching street theater at NYU. So fab to see you, lovey, what's going in your life?"

I told her about the book of erotic stories I'm writing and my teaching job.

"You hanging out with a bloke now?" she wanted to know.

"No, I just got dumped by a jerk," I answered.

"Maybe I can console you," Sophie said, and she grabbed my hand and put it on her fat, full breast. "Here, have a squeeze," she said, "for old time's sake."

"Knock, knock," I said, pulling at her big brown nipple as if it were a door knocker.

"Who's there?" she said.

"Me," I answered.

"Me, me who?" was her inevitable reply.

"Meet me in the garden," I answered. We both laughed.

"You are as silly as ever," she said. I pulled her nipple again, but before I could make a habit of it, someone tapped me on the back.

I turned and there was Ron Jeremy, naked, with his big pink wanker sticking out from his crotch like an arrow. For a second I thought I was back in my dream, but then I realized it was a man wearing a pair of joke Groucho Marx glasses with the attached nose, and a flesh-colored bodysuit with a big cloth dick sewn on.

"Excuse me," he said, "I'm making a very experimental film. Would you two beauties like to try out the casting couch? Come with me, darlings, and experience the motion of the ocean." I recognized the voice right away; it was Murphy.

"Oh Murph," I said. "You read the *TONY* article, too."

"You betcha. . . . I'm so glad you made it, what do you think of the party?"

"Mellow as rainbow Jell-O," I told him. "You must have written the guidelines."

"Who else? I am the Emily Post of sex parties," he said. "So," Murphy said, his false nose quivering, "you have met Sophie of the heavenly hooters. . . ."

"Actually we are old friends," I told him.

"Well, kittens, Jeremy must put on the feed bag. Don't do anything I wouldn't do," said Murphy, as he moved toward the kitchen.

"That leaves us a field bigger than the planet Jupiter," I said to Sophie.

"Let's look around," Sophie said. "I want to check out what's happening on the stage." We made our way toward the back of the room holding hands. As we got closer to the stage I heard catcalls, whistles. Someone yelled out, "Oh baby, hit her again." Finally we inched our way to the front of the crowd so we had a clear view.

Two tall, opulent women occupied the spotlight, their bodies massive as marble statues of goddesses. One was wearing a black nylon bra and panties, and over the panties a long, thick, yellow rubber strap-on. The other woman wore nothing at all. The nude woman was bent over a small red velvet settee that was in the center of the stage. Her big breasts spilled out from under her arms. Using the flat of her hand, the standing woman rhythmically hit her kneeling friend, first on one buttock, then the other. With each blow, the supine woman cried out, "Oh, Daddy, please, hit me again." Both cheeks of her humongous ass were so crimson they were almost purple. The spanking must have been going on for a long time.

I found myself leaning back against Sophie as we watched. She had one arm across my chest. Her other arm magically found its way up under my short skirt, and her hand moved between my legs. She slipped a finger inside the elastic of my scanty panties and gently probed between my labia to find my little clit. I wasn't wet yet, but slowly, as reverentially as if it was the ring of the pope, she stroked and stroked me. Soon my clit moistened, swelled, and got so wet that the sacred moisture spread through the pretty cathedral between my legs. Sophie put a second, third, fourth finger inside me, and I rocked back and forth on her hand as she kept inching up within me. Meanwhile, on the stage, the woman was shrieking louder and louder. The sex juice was running down my thighs, between my knees. I didn't care if it flooded the floor. As I moved forward to get better leverage, I noticed the woman next to me was bending over, coddling and stroking her neighbor's engorged cock while he had a hand out, caressing her breast. Back and forth, back and forth, I rocked on Sophie's hand. I was breathing harder; she was working me, I was letting go, then Sophie inched her thumb inside me and I was over the top. As I came, I yelled, "Oh, oh, oh . . . ," so loudly that the people around us turned to look.

We rested quietly for a minute, then Sophie said into my ear, "It's so wonderful to touch you again." I nodded and stepped forward a bit and she slid her hand out from under my skirt.

Meanwhile up on the stage, the spanking stopped. The woman in the dildo helped the other woman up from the settee. She was shaky, trembling, but her face was glowing with pleasure, and I thought she must have just come, too. Very ceremoniously the woman who had been doing the spanking took the strap-on off and buckled it around the hips of her friend. The audience cheered as the women clasped hands, bowed, and walked off the stage.

Sophie nuzzled my neck; she whispered, "That was great fun. Our meeting tonight must be fate, karma. We were meant to be together. Let's go away this weekend. I have some money saved." Her eagerness scared me.

"I don't know," I mumbled, and then lamely, inanely, "these things happen at parties." I put my hand out and touched her arm, but then I moved a step away. I felt unhappy, my postorgasmic glow dissipating quickly into the blue light. Suddenly I thought about three-inch Sam, perfidious three-inch Sam, how happy I used to feel when I knew he was coming over. My thoughts were interrupted by a few loud bars of "Roll Out the Barrel."

Ron Jeremy/Murphy bounded out onto the stage. He was wearing a big, white cowboy hat. "Attention, attention, friends and revelers," he said. "We have a very special act making a debut tonight, a newly formed country-western dance troupe rustling up their Lusty Loft brand of pleasure. Let's have a great big hand for the Cobble Hill Cowpokes." He picked up the settee and carried it off-stage to loud applause. Four men wearing cowboy hats, cowboy boots, and jockstraps trotted into view. The leader of the troupe was holding a rope coiled in his hand. The second man up onstage was three-inch Sam. The leader twirled his lasso above his head. "Yippee, tii, yi, yippee ti-yi, get along little doggies," he yodeled. The three other men did a cute shuffle-off-to-Buffalo, and then turned, put their hands on the floor, and pushed up their bottoms, in an approximation of the downward dog position in yoga.

My head was boiling with confusion. I wanted to take my brain out and wash it under cold clean water, but I could not take my eyes off the stage. I watched the Cobble Hill Cowpokes shaking their shapely, tight bottoms from side to side. Was this why he broke it off? The other "people" he wanted to go with were guys! Why couldn't he just tell me? He knew all my secrets. He knew about my false front teeth, my padded bras. We had never talked about my going with women, but he had seen the strap-on in my toy drawer. He had read my story, "Athena, Hunter of Women." How could he not have guessed? I wondered if I would be able to accept his being with other men, even though I knew that if he bedded another woman it would drive me berserk. I know that no one can ever own another person, but I have always been so possessive. Would I become just as competitive if my lover was screwing a man? But why, what is the difference? I would really have to go deep inside my baroque and tortured brain to figure this one out. The cowpokes, standing up again and facing the audience, were now doing a cancan. I had never noticed that Sam had such great legs.

I felt that lovely familiar moisture bubbling up again between my thighs, where Sophie's fingers had been only a few minutes ago. The cowpokes turned their heads to the left, then to the right as they kick-stepped. Sam looked directly at me; he broke pace and stumbled, his face darkened, and he was blushing. He had seen me.

Sophie touched my shoulder; I had forgotten that she was even standing beside me. "What's the matter? You look like you've seen a ghost," she said, and she put her arm protectively around me. "Let's go get something to eat; the food looked yummy." It wasn't food I wanted. I wanted to talk to Sam.

I moved out from under her arm. I felt like a shit, but I knew she wasn't right for me. "I'm sorry, Sophie, I can't go on with this. It won't work for me," I said. Her eyes filled with tears and the corners of her mouth turned down. Her hands clenched into fists.

For a minute I thought she was going to punch me, and I wouldn't have blamed her. Instead, she spat out, "At least you got your jollies off, you cunt-teasing bitch." She whirled around, flinging her arms wide like a furious dervish, and ran into the crowd.

Back on the stage, the man with the lariat had just lassoed a miserable-looking Sam around the neck. Sam was staring at me while doing a sloppy two-step. As I returned to the watching crowd, I felt the whole room rock beneath my feet; it was the motion of the ocean rolling under me.

Diamond Earrings

It was eleven-thirty P.M. and the heat was off. I was in bed under the covers watching Johnny Carson and lightly diddling myself when the phone rang. I didn't want to leave my warm nest, but I forced myself to get it. No one had phoned me for days.

It was Lionheart. "What are you doing now? Can I come over?" he asked with no preliminaries, as if we had seen each other yesterday. I hadn't seen him in over a year. Right after Nixon resigned, Lionheart took me to CBGB's in a stretch limo to hear this new band, the Ramones. I wore the white crocheted lace dress he had brought back from Mexico. When we got back to my place after the show, he peeled the dress and my underthings off me and laid me naked right down in the middle of my bedroom rug. With his finger, he traced a white lace design down my body with the fine white powder he had in a little glass vial. He put some of the white powder in my nose, and then he took off all his clothes, sat next to me on the rug, and erased the design grain by grain with his tongue. So much sweet water poured out between my legs that I thought we were going to float out the window. We fucked till dawn and never made it off the rug to the bed.

"Yes, you can come over," I told him.

"Right away?" he asked.

"Give me an hour," I said. "The Dallas Cowboys are here. I have to get rid of them."

I thought I heard him snicker. "Sure," he said, then hung up the phone.

I had heard he was in Lima, in Amsterdam, in Tangier, but I would never ask. We no longer had a commitment, and even if we did, I didn't want to be the kind of person who keeps tabs, just like I didn't want anyone keeping tabs on me. Though the truth was, even with everything that had happened, if he had said once again that he wanted to be with me alone, and if he asked once again if I would be his one and only, I would have said yes without missing a breath. He was still my prince, my phoenix, my pleasure pie.

I dashed out of bed into the shower. At least there was hot water. I washed my hair, my body, and the thick patch between my legs with Dr. Bronner's Almond Soap. I wanted to smell like marzipan all over. I changed the sheets on the bed, took the dirty dishes out of the sink, and put them in the back of the closet. He loved me in velvet, so I put on my red velvet shirt with the ruffled sleeves, jeans, and my embroidered Chinese slippers. I was drying my hair when the bell rang. I wrapped the towel around my head, ran down the stairs, and flung open the door.

He was leaning against the black Lincoln Continental idling at the curb. As soon as Lionheart saw me, he tapped the window of the car and it sped away. In two giant steps, he was inside the hallway. He picked me up under the arms and held me high in the air like I was a baby, then I locked my legs around his waist. He carried me up the four flights of stairs like that.

I had left the door wide open. He charged in right through the kitchen, into the next room, and put me down on the bed. He went and locked the door, then came back to sit beside me.

"I missed you," he said. His forehead was sweating and his breath was labored. I remembered when he used to throw me over his shoulder and carry me up the stairs like I was a sack of potatoes.

"I missed you, too," I said. His face was puffy, fuller, and the skin was now a little slack under his chin. I wondered if he was noticing all the tiny pigeon tracks on my upper lip and the two new vertical lines across my forehead.

He grabbed me and pulled me to him. "Beautiful as ever," he said. He kissed my neck, rested his chin on my shoulder. The towel had fallen from my head. My mass of hair cascaded down over us, holding us safe together in a fragrant net. The ratcheting sound of his breath slowed. I put my cheek against his; he needed a shave but I didn't care.

"I have something for you," Lionheart said. He took a small packet wrapped in tissue paper out of his inside coat pocket, then he shrugged the coat off and let it fall to the floor. He handed the packet to me. When I opened it, a pair of perfect, large diamond earrings, marquise cut, sparkled on my palm. They were dazzling, sending rays of sparkling light into the far corners of the room. I wanted him to think I was a tough girl, but despite myself I started to cry.

"What's the matter," he said. "You would have preferred emeralds?"

"You're a funny guy," I told him. "They're fantastic. I'm stunned."

"Well, stop bawling and put them on. Here, I'll do it," he said, and moved toward me. I could smell the booze on him, the familiar, ripe corn smell of Jack Daniel's. He put the earrings in, pulling down the lobes of my ears so as not to hurt me, and pushed the hair back from my face.

"You got the screw backs so you can't lose them. Go look at yourself, Rita Hayworth," he told me. "You're gorgeous." I got up and looked at myself in the mirror over my dresser. The shining diamonds made my face look so radiant, so alive.

"Thank you, thank you, I always wanted diamond earrings," I told him. I was strong enough to fight the urge to ask him if this meant we were engaged. Instead, I said, "And you, you look like a movie star, too; you look better than Sean Connery, that is if Sean Connery was a blond, in *Live and Let Die*."

I was lying. Even though he was smiling at me, he looked tired and sad. "Here," I said, going to him. "You need to relax." I pushed his body down on the bed. He clasped his hands behind his head with a grateful sigh. I unbuckled his belt, pulled down his zipper, put my hands inside his boxers in search of my dear old friend. It was limp in my hand as I pulled it free. Lionheart was uncut, and I bent my head to kiss the lovely, pointy tip. There was a funny, strange odor coming off it, somewhere between mustard and rubber. I asked myself if he would have come to me right after being with someone else, without even washing. Then I asked myself if it mattered. Maybe I was jumping to conclusions; what difference did it make?

I noticed he was shaking in the chilly room. "It's cold in here and you're shivering," I said. "Don't go away, I'm going to give you a nice, warm wash." I pulled the quilt up around him.

"You're a good kid, a great kid," he said. I went to the bathroom, got a washcloth, and moistened it with warm water.

When I came back to him, he was sitting up; there was a large silver compact open on the bed. I watched as he chopped the white crystals on the mirror into thin lines with a single-edge razor blade. Then he took the hundred-dollar bill that was resting on the sheet and rolled it into a tight cylinder. He held it out to me.

"A little toot?" he asked. I took it, bent my head over the compact, and snorted the thinner of the two white lines up into my nose. It burned though the back of my throat and down my spine, making my body tingle all the way to my toes. Instantly, everything in the room became so clear and shiny, glistening. Lionheart did up his line, then he licked the mirror and put the paraphernalia back into the compact. He put it on the bedside table. He lay back on the bed, spread his arms wide. "Do with me what you will," he said.

When I wrapped the washcloth around his long sex, he smiled. "Feels great," he said. I washed him gently from base to tip. The hair around his meaty balls was all matted, so I got up to get my comb. I came back, combed the tangles out, and washed his golden thatch some more. When the weird odor was gone, I started to wash him with my tongue. Slowly I moved from the base of his cock to the tip, up and down, down and up, but the little hood did not pull back to reveal his cockhead. I teased, sucked, put hand my under his balls, bouncing them in my palm in a way I knew he loved. I continued all this for a long time, hours, days, centuries. I got a crick in my neck, but I kept on, still his cock was soft and limp. I got up, stripped, then I bent my bosoms over his face. "Lick between my tits," I said, "get them real wet." He put out his tongue and licked the little valley between my breasts, but without much vigor.

"Now take your trigger finger and stick it up my ass," I told him. He closed his eyes and did as I asked.

I bent over, catching his cock between my breasts, holding it there, then moving on him, cuddling it between my tits like a shy worm. Even this did not excite him. I soon found myself rubbing my skin against his zipper and scratching myself. I looked up; his eyes were wide open. "I'm sorry, I'm sorry, babe," he said.

"No, no," I told him. "Don't worry." I got up and took off his shoes and socks, trousers, underwear, and shirt. Then I put my whole body down on him. I moved my hips, trying to caress him with my silky, hairy vulva. I started to kiss him, using my tongue like a little cock moving in and out of his mouth. The room was growing darker, collapsing in on us.

Lionheart pulled his mouth away from mine. He put his hand up under my hair, raising my head.

"Stop trying to be such a hero," he said. "I'm just too beat. I've been traveling for days. I have a red in my pocket. I'll split it with you, and we can both get some sleep. How about it?" he asked.

I felt a sudden intense pressure behind my eyes; a dense cloud of tears had gathered there. I blinked, trying to expel them, but I could not. My eyes burned, hot and dry. "Okay," I said.

When I woke up, the room was filled with sunlight. The clock next to the bed said one-ten. It was already afternoon. Lionheart was not in bed. He was up and dressed in the kitchen, fussing with the coffee things.

"Good morning," I called out to him. "I mean, good afternoon."

"Get out of bed, you lazy broad. You can see I'm making coffee; get dressed. I want to go out."

"Er, uugh," I said. I felt groggy; my mouth was sore from all that sucking. "Only if you bring the coffee to me in bed," I told him.

"You drive a hard bargain," he answered when he brought our coffees in on the black lacquer tray my mother had given me. He set the tray down on the bed, sat down, and handed me my cup.

"So," I said, "where do you want to go?"

"Where we go all the time," he answered, "to the top of the World Trade Center, then we'll come back to Brooklyn and go for lunch at Gage and Tollner's."

There were white caps on the river; it looked very cold out, so I wore my new shearling coat from Afghanistan. It smelled like goats. We walked over the bridge holding hands. When we got to the World Trade Center, we had to wait in a long line just to get in the elevator. Several of the people around us sniffed loudly, probably smelling my coat. We strolled around the observation deck. Lionheart liked to come here because he said he liked the feeling that the world was at his feet.

"From the neck down you look like a hippie chick," Lionheart said, "but from the neck up, wearing those earrings, you look high society."

"Thanks for the high part," I told him. "I don't know about the society." I still felt kind of whacked out, but at least I no longer felt groggy. The air was so clear it was like being on top of a mountain. There wasn't a cloud in the sky, not even over New Jersey. We paused on the Brooklyn side. I liked to look across the river because I could actually see my building, a tiny gray box under the Brooklyn Bridge.

He put an arm around my shoulder. "I wonder if I'll always live there," I said.

"Maybe one day you'll live with me on a tropical island and all we'll do is eat coconuts and make love," he said. I thought he must have been feeling bad about last night.

"Sounds great," I said.

"Seriously," he said, "it must be seven years, since we know each other. What would you like to be doing five years from now?"

I corrected him. "Eight years and two months."

"You got a better mind than I do," he said, "that's for sure."

"No," I told him, "it's because everything about you is unforgettable. Anyhow, I'll just be happy if in five years from now someone starts publishing my poems. I could wallpaper my bathroom with the rejection slips."

"It'll happen," he said, "you just gotta keep at it."

"I hope so," I answered, "but where do you want to be in five years?"

"If I live that long," he said.

"Don't ever talk like that," I said, my voice becoming shrill. "I can't stand it. Now tell me where you want to be. . . ."

"I got some capital accumulated," he said. "Maybe I'll buy property in Woodstock, open a bar, start painting again." I had heard this kind of talk before. The last time it was a restaurant in Key West, before that a hotel in Provincetown. "Then I'll write my memoirs, and you'll come up and edit them."

"No, thanks," I said. "I only want to do my own work."

He grinned, making his face so handsome. "Aren't you tough? Aren't you the tough guy? Let's go for oysters," he said, and he lightly punched my arm.

I didn't want to leave this celestial realm and go back down into the pits of life, but I was very hungry. "You got a deal," I answered.

Despite the cold, people were enjoying the sun, sitting on the steps in front of the building, talking and eating. Lionheart said, "You up for walking back over the bridge?"

"I'd walk to a desert island with you," I told him.

Gage and Tollner's was, thankfully, only a short walk from the bridge. This old restaurant, complete with genuine Victorian decor, serves seafood, cooked southern style. Diamond Jim Brady and Boss Tweed were rumored to have eaten here.

"Do you think you could eat two dozen Gulf Coast oysters?" Lionheart asked when we were seated at a table by the window.

"Do fish swim in the sea?" I said. He told the waiter to bring us two dozen each. In the end, I could manage only eighteen; he finished the other six. We had crabmeat Virginia and split a bottle of white wine that cost fifty-eight dollars.

"Only top shelf for you, kiddo," he said as he ordered it.

By the time we got back to my place the winter sun was setting, a great red ball sinking behind the Statue of Liberty. We stood together at the window and watched it slip into the ocean as the sky deepened into nighttime blue.

"Those earrings are so bright, we don't need to turn the lights on," said Lionheart.

"I adore them," I told him. "I'm never taking them off."

"If you're ever strapped for cash," he said, "you could sell them for a nice piece of change." I told him that I would never sell them. "I hope you never have to," he said. "How's your job going? You need a little extra?"

I worked weekends tending bar at a club in trendy new Tribeca. "I'm fine," I said.

"Then let me leave you my stash," he went on. "I've got plenty."

"No, no thanks, I'm fine," I repeated. I was trying to wean myself from the stuff. I didn't like the way it ate up my time, left me weak and scattered, unable to do much the next day.

"You sure?" he said.

"Yeah," I answered, "absolutely."

"Independent and stubborn as ever," he said, "but that's what endears you to me. Come on." He took my hand and led me to the other room. He sat me on the bed and started to unlace my Doc Martens. He didn't say a word until all my clothes were off. Then he undid his pants and pulled it out, already up and eager. He bent over, poked me in the crotch with it. "This is for you," he said. "See what you do to me." Then he peeled off the rest of his clothes. I loved the way he was hung, how he swung low and to the left. His foreskin was already drawing back, exposing his purple cockhead. I put my hand up and grabbed him. I spread wide, lifted my legs up in a V. Then I pulled him right down into my oh-so-hungry hole. He was my phoenix again, burning into me, rising up again and again. His arms on either side of my hips, he kept pushing into me, deeper and deeper. I thought he was going to split me in two, but I didn't want him to stop; I wrapped my ankles around his neck, opened to him so completely I was inside out. We always came together and it was always the best, at first like exploding pyrotechnics of pure delight and then like floating in the ocean on the hottest night in July.

We rested, I pushed my nose into his armpit; I liked the musty smell of his sweat. His cock softened and slid out, but he was still on top. I didn't mind the weight of him.

Finally he said, "Jesus, what time is it?" I glanced at the clock on the bed table.

"Eight-thirty," I told him.

He jumped up, "I have to get out of here. I need to shower," he said.

"Sure," I said. "You know where everything is."

Twenty minutes later he was dressed and bending over me, smelling of Dr. Bonner's soap. He kissed me, a long kiss, giving me one last taste of that sugar mouth. "Take care of yourself," he told me.

"You, too," I said, and then he was out the door. I listened to his footsteps hurrying away down the hall.

It was freezing in the room, another chilly night with no heat. I didn't have the energy to get up and turn on the TV. I pulled the covers high around my neck and started to roll over on my belly. I always like to sleep like that. I felt a sharp, small tug at the back of my head as if a ghostly imp was pulling my hair. I put my hand up behind my ear to find a long strand of hair was tangled up in the screw back of my earring, forming a tight, little knot.

Geezer Love

Marina comes to visit after a month spent in Amsterdam. She brings me a pair of shiny, red rubber panties with no crotch. She says to me that there is a big demand for old lady porn in the sex shops over there. "What do you mean, old lady porn?" I ask her. "Porn for old ladies?" But I'm only pulling her chain because I know what she means. I've visited the Sultry Senior Slutizens site on the web several times.

"No, no," she says, and she passes the lit joint back across the table to me. "Pictures of old ladies completely starkers or in negligees or you know," she explains, "just bare ass to the camera, bent over, their faces smiling out between their open legs, or even the classic—plain, wide-open, spread pussy." She spreads her thighs wide to illustrate and hooks one long, elegant, leather-panted leg over the arm of her chair.

"When I last visited Amsterdam," she goes on, "you'd find a few old lady mags on a rack way in the back of the sex shops with esoteric stuff like *Busty Bearded Beauties*. Now the same magazines are on the racks in the front. They put them right on the counter by the cash register next to bestsellers like *Buns of Glory* and *Lesbian Love Triangles.*"

"How old are these women?" I ask her. "In their sixties? That's not so old," I say. I'm just the other side of fifty.

"No, no, no, they're really up there," she answers. "Seventy, maybe even eighty."

"Why this sudden rage for over-the-hill dames in Tulipland?" I want to know.

"Maybe it's because their queen is no spring chicken. They utterly idolize her. They are such loyal people," she says. "Or maybe it's because it's so way out, one of the last taboos, like fixating on your grandma."

I take a long drag as I digest this information. "You mean," I ask, "in Holland fucking your brother isn't naughty anymore?"

"You're a laugh riot," she says. "But anyhow, now in Amsterdam, when you go to a club, you see all these old ladies out partying and getting chatted up by young studs."

"Maybe I'll move there," I say.

After she leaves, I go back to my writing, but I can't concentrate. Visions of skanky-legged old women in fishnets and garters float through my brain. When I was at the Tunnel last month, an old lady was getting a whipping. She looked seventy, her face criss-crossed with deep lines, her blue hair pulled back into a ponytail. She was wearing only a black satin bustier and red spike heels. She was being flogged with a braided cat-o'-nine-tails by a pretty, big-titted blonde wench in a maid's outfit. With every stroke of the whip, loose flesh on the old woman's thighs jiggled, but still she had a fine Rubenesque figure. She looked good. She was smiling and panting at the same time, her face suffused with ecstasy. There were three or four guys in leather jodhpurs or studded jeans standing around with their cocks out, wanking away. Looking at her, I wondered what I'd be doing for pleasure in fifteen years.

The memories of the woman, the smells of sweat and leather, the dimly lit, smoky club peopled with shifting, moving forms get me excited. My own rank smell wafts up from between my legs.

I go to my lingerie drawer, where I keep my two battery-operated vibrators. I had named the ribbed purple plastic one "Glory of God," and the long, thin, green one "Lionheart," after the love of my life. I decide that Lionheart will pilot me this time. Even after I am all lubed up and we are flying into the clouds, the vision of the blue-haired old lady flickers and burns behind my eyes.

The next day, as I drink my morning coffee, I am still thinking about old lady porn. There must be old man porn, too, but I have never seen any. I have never even been to bed with any old men. I never did it with anyone older than forty-nine, and that was with Louis Lanza when I was twenty. He would stand beside the bed drinking Old Crow from the bottle, looking at me lying naked on his bed until he was ready to thrust his meaty tool between my thighs. I wonder if he's still alive somewhere, maybe snoozing in a wheelchair in a nursing home, dreaming about my little pink legs waving in the air. I have nothing against old guys, but I never seem to meet any. My last affair was with a guy who was thirty-two. I broke it off because he wanted me to suck him all the time, but he would never go down on me.

I dress and prepare to take the subway to Manhattan—I have to go to the Strand and pick up some books for the erotic literature class I teach. On the number 4 train there is a heavyset, graying, older guy sitting across from me. He looks like Jean Gabin in *Wages of Fear*. I wonder if he is wearing a peach-color lace bra and panties beneath his business suit. His thighs are so beefy that they strain against the fabric of his slacks. I wonder if he has a big, beefy set of balls to match, so big they can be seen peeping out beneath the elastic of his panties. I decide to wink at him as I get off the train at Fourteenth Street. He pulls his head back as if I'd slapped him.

Once inside the Strand, I make a beeline for the Erotica section, a meager two shelves below a bargain counter in the very back of the store. There was the usual: *Story of O,* Frank Harris's *My Life and Loves, Lolita, Candy, Vox.* But I am looking for, and can't find, a cut-rate *Macho Sluts.* Still, it is nice to be kneeling here under the counter in this dark grotto of truth-speaking books. I want to open my mouth and stroke the spine of each book with my tongue. I remember that I want to check the art section for an Egon Schiele book. I stand up quickly and bump into someone. I have butted a bald, stout old guy with a scraggly, gray beard and mustache. He has an armload of books; the top one is *How I Became One of the Invisible.* "I'm sorry," I say.

"That's okay," the man answers. As I turn away, he says," Wait, could it be, could it be, Colette, is that you?"

"Well, yeah," I say, "but do I know you?"

"I know I've changed, but you, you're still a knockout. I'd recognize you anywhere," he says.

I don't know who this old geezer is, but I'm beginning to like him. I take a closer look; there is something about the way his big ears stand out, like the handles of a cup, that is familiar. Under the wispy mustache, his lips are full and purple, as if filled with dark blood. This mouth I know; it belongs to Charley Cummings. This mouth has been everywhere on my body. His tongue has been inside my every orifice. He would even pull it out of my mouth and snake it into my nostril and root around. I was still a college girl when he, a photographer, fifteen years my senior, picked me up in the biography section of the Grand Army Plaza Library. He extracted a promise of fidelity and pledged eternal love. Six months after we met, I found out he was balling his ex-wife, Patty, on the nights he said he was going to see his headshrinker.

He had a long pink dick. As it got big and hard it used to curve. It would peek out at me, rising from the light brown thicket of his pubic hair like a worm emerging from its lair. I liked to lift my head as he loomed above me and watch it crawl into me. I remember my rage when I found out about him and Patty. I wanted to cut that worm off. I wanted to bury it beneath a tree in Prospect Park so it could burrow its way to hell.

"Are you okay?" he says.

"Charley," I answer, coming back to the now, "it's been such a long time. How are you doing?" I'm not about to tell him I'd been visualizing his amputated cock.

"Very good, working hard," he said. "I have a studio up in Inwood now. I ran into Harriet at a Dave Van Ronk concert; she told me you'd become a writer. You look great." You, I think, you look like you've been spending your days in porno theaters.

"Come have a coffee with me," he says. "We have a lot of catching up to do."

"Why, why do we have to catch up at all?" I shoot back. I am surprised at my nasty tone. Could I still be carrying a grudge after so many years? Maybe I was becoming bitter? I remembered the bearded man I met at Tonic last week. He was wearing a thick, gold marriage band. "Hi," he said, and then with no further preliminaries, "aren't you going to invite me over to your place; we could have some fun."

I sputtered out, "But you're married . . ."

"Ah, come on," he said, "you're older, you take it when you can get it; you should know the score."

"Go home to your wife, poor woman," I told him.

Now Charley was looking at me imploringly. "I've thought of you so often over the years," he says. "Oh, come on, it's just coffee." I notice he has what looks like a piece of spinach stuck between his two front teeth. His personal hygiene had never been the best.

"No, no, I don't think so," I say.

For a second he looks hurt, then he bounces right back. He smiles and pulls his wallet out of his jeans pocket. "At least take my card," he says, "give me a call. I know you must think about me sometimes, too." He always was a cocky bastard. I take the card automatically. "Well, it was wonderful seeing you," he says. He turns quickly on his heel and goes toward the cashier.

When I get home, I find a message on my answering machine from my editor, Clothilde, at *Open Door* magazine. She says the last story that I sent her lacked punch. You seem to be repeating yourself, she says, the sex scenes are almost exactly like the ones in "Fatima of Fifth Street." No wonder, I think as I listen to her message, I haven't gotten laid for six months. I'm beginning to feel like a phony, a sex writer who doesn't have sex. Maybe I should call up Charley; maybe he was sent to inspire me. I have a vision of his long pink cock again, this time it is pointing straight up, a thick finger beckoning me. I realize that the call from Clothilde has really upset me, made me feel threatened and desperate. I remember all the times in the past when I jumped into bed with someone because I felt that way. It was always a disaster. I should wait, not do anything rash, calm down, relax. I drink a water glass full of scotch and retire to my bed with the Glory of God rather than Lionheart. I want to relate to the cosmos and not be reminded of an old love. The glory of God is granted to me twice, but I can't help missing, even as I am coming, the real thing, the feeling of skin on skin, the soft hot tissue of life. As I am drifting off into the dream world, I decide that tomorrow I will call Charley.

I phone him at noon. He sounds surprised when he hears my voice. That makes me happy, maybe he isn't so sure of himself after all. "I was really hoping you would phone," he says, "I was thinking of you all last night."

"What were you thinking?" I want to know.

"I was thinking how sweet you have always been and what an idiot I was."

"Yes," I said, "you were an idiot." I didn't want to make it too easy for him.

"Look, how about coming up here for dinner tonight? I want you to see what I'm working on." I lie and tell him I am busy. "Well, how about tomorrow then?" he asks.

"Okay," I say, and I write down his address.

It is a long ride up to his place at the very top of Manhattan. At 125th Street the subway goes above ground. The buildings I see out the window look ancient and baroque. Following Charley's instructions, I get off at 207th Street and walk north up Tenth Avenue. I can see the low hills of the Bronx rising across the river just two blocks away. I find his building, an ancient colossus that has seen better days. Climbing the six flights of stairs to his top-floor apartment, I smell food on every landing, curry, onions, ribs, frying fish.

He flings open the door as soon as I knock. He is wearing clean jeans and a clean white shirt. His scraggly beard and mustache have been neatly trimmed. He smiles wide, and I can see that his teeth had been cleaned, too. "Thank you," he says as he takes the bag I offer to him.

"It's sake," I say.

"I just love sake; somehow you always do the right thing," he answers.

"You're buttering me up before I'm even in the door, Charley," I tell him. "You haven't changed."

I walk into a large, spacious room with windows on two sides. Cut into one wall is a doorway that leads to the room beyond. It is the remaining wall that is so amazing. That wall is entirely covered, from floor to ceiling, with photos of women's faces. The women aren't models or pretty girls, but they aren't young either. They look to be my age or older, even much older. The women are all smiling or laughing. I can see the lines, the age spots, the circles under their eyes, but all the women look beautiful, rich, and alive.

"I call it *Real Women*," Charley says. "In this youth-worshipping culture, I'm a freak. I think women are so beautiful when the life they have lived shows on their faces. Of course I would be lying if I didn't say I still find young women attractive, too."

It occurs to me that with him I wouldn't feel the need to pluck out my white pubic hairs. I do not share this thought with him. What I say is, "You're just a hound, Charley; you always were."

"Except, I've learned my lesson," he answers. "I can only handle one at a time."

"I don't believe everything you say the way I used to, Charley," I tell him. He looks down, suddenly shamefaced.

"I'm really sorry," he says. "You know people can change. Anyhow, these women all live in this neighborhood. The pictures are for a show next month in Atlanta."

"It's great, very positive, so full of joy and life. I love it," I tell him.

He is so pleased, his eyes sparkle. "I'm working harder now than ever," he says. "I feel the pressure of time and all that, but you know it's not so bad, it's good. How about you? You always wanted to be a writer, and you found your way. I'm delighted; you must tell me all about your work over dinner. Everything is ready."

He leads me into the kitchen, pulls out a chair, and seats me ceremoniously. A big pot of chili on a hot plate is ready on the table. He pours us full glasses of sake and then ladles generous portions of chili into white porcelain bowls. It tastes fantastic. He tells me about the last show he'd had. It was in Cuba. The country is so poor, he says, he always paid more than the asking price when he bought something. Then he gets personal; he wants to know if memories of our trysts have inspired me in my erotic writings.

I answer that I barely remember.

I still sound angry, he says, and then, "I can understand that, but I'm just so happy you weren't still too pissed off to come up to dinner."

As he clears table, I couldn't help noticing that, despite his girth, his haunches seem solid and firm. "How old are you now?" I ask him. "You're not in bad shape for a veritable geezer."

"I'm sixty-seven," he answers, "and besides, I don't get older, I get better, just like you."

I tell him, "Flattery will get you nowhere," but I am lying. His charm is getting to me.

"Let's sit on that couch in my studio and have an after-dinner brandy," he says. "Go sit down. I'll bring the drinks in."

I go into the other room and sit on the lumpy, old blue sofa. The setting sun streams through the windows, making the smiling faces shine. I know he is going to make a move on me, and I feel frightened. I feel like getting up and dashing out the door, but the smiling women whisper, Nothing ventured, nothing gained.

What could possibly happen that hasn't happened before? I ask myself. Then I think about how I couldn't stand to be hurt again. I am only a few feet from the door. I can whisk away so quickly he won't hear me. Just at that moment, he comes into the room holding the brandy snifters. It is already too late.

He hands me mine and sits down on the couch, leaving some space between us. He takes a big gulp of his brandy.

"This brandy smells too good to be gulped down," I say.

"I know," he answers, "but I'm nervous. I think you're terrific. Please believe I'm so sorry for what happened long ago, and maybe," he says slowly, shyly turning his face toward me, "maybe we could really cook now."

Now it is I who take a big swallow of brandy. "I don't know if I'm still angry, but I'm frightened," I say. I don't tell him that I don't find his balding head or his bulky body exciting. I gulp down the rest of the brandy and look into Charley's eyes. They are clear, as clear as a boy's. I look down at his large, callused, well-shaped hands.

"Er, ah . . ." I start to say, still feeling ambivalent, hedging for time, then I belch my brandy breath right in his face. He takes this for a come-hither sign because he leans over and kisses me with real passion. His mouth is hungry, fresh as the mouth of a young Kerouac, bold as the mouth of a young Neal Cassady. His tongue is deep inside my mouth, and I feel myself responding, getting wet between my legs. Then, just like Joey Gavino used to do behind the handball court in tenth grade, Charley slips his hand into the waistband of my skirt, inside the elastic of my panties. He reaches down to put two thick fingers inside my cunt so he is kissing me and finger-fucking me at the same time. With his other hand he cups my breast, and his fingers pull steadily at my nipple. His fingers inside me carry me along, move with me as my body starts to move, my hips dancing in pleasure until I come.

"Okay?" he asks. "Are you okay?" I tell him that I feel great, and then he kisses me sweetly and covers me with his body like a big warm blanket. I can feel the weight of his big belly spreading over me. I don't mind. I want to feel him skin to skin. I pull my jersey and bra off over my head and fling them on the floor, and then I unbutton his shirt and peel it off. His once generous chest hair is sparse and white, only a few tufts remaining around his nipples. I used to love the thick mat on his chest. I would tug at it with my teeth playfully as we fucked. My face must register my disappointment because he says, "Everything changes." He tries a laugh, but instead a weak "He . . . he, he, he," comes out. "As life goes on we must deal with changes," he says.

The last thing I want right then is to get involved in a philosophical conversation. "Oh you, why don't you just shut up and suck my tittie," I say. This time he does laugh, and then he fastens his thick lips to my nipple and sucks. Having my nipples sucked has always driven me wild, the nerves at the end of my tits must be attached to my clit. Hot, rolling waves of bliss ripple down from my breast, soaking my pussy. I want him inside me.

I push my skirt and panties down in obvious invitation, but he keeps sucking away. He has turned into one big suck machine. Since he doesn't take the hint, my hands go for his fly and zip down. To my surprise, he pushes my hand away.

"What happened?" I say. "What's wrong?"

He disentangles himself from me and sits up. His lower lip is trembling, and he looks as if he is going to cry. "What is it, what's going on?" I want to know.

"I, uh, uh, I . . . it's so, so, so. I don't know what it is . . . but I have to tell you, I—"

"What is it?" I yell. "Do you have a disease or something?"

He mumbles, "No, it's not something like that, not exactly, but it's just— Oh what the hell," he goes on. "Just look." He pulls his pants and briefs down to his knees. His cock is all curled up like a sleeping snail. With all the making out we'd been doing, I am surprised that it isn't at all hard. "I have this condition," he says. "It happens when men get older. The valves in your balls weaken, so you don't get erect." He puts a finger down against his leg behind his scrotum, and he makes a pushing, in-out, in-out motion. Suddenly his cock perks up. It swells, stretching right out before my eyes. It grows into that long old worm I remember.

I jump back, startled. "Jesus Christ, what was that?" I exclaim. I have just entered the twilight zone. "I know it's a shock," he says, "but I got an implant, a little pump, surgically inserted inside my thigh, that does the work my valves can't do anymore. I still feel like a young man; I'm not ready to hang up my spurs. Now it will be hard for at least an hour."

"Well, wow," I say, almost nonplussed. I had certainly never seen anything like this before. This was something new. I reach out and touch it gingerly, like it is an alien creature, but beneath my fingers it feels like good old hot, hard cock. I squeeze it, and it remains firm in my hand. "Can you . . . come?" I ask him. "Oh, sure, absolutely, just like before, and if I don't want to come after a half hour or so, I just squeeze it again and see," he says, reaching between his legs once more, "I can make it go down." He makes the pushing motion, and his erection subsides. "Anyhow, I can go for hours, that is if I don't throw my back out." He is smiling now. Oh no, I think, this guy is falling apart.

"What, so you have a bad back, too?" I ask him.

"No, no, I was just making a joke," he says.

"Very funny," I reply, but I am feeling calmer. *A bird in the hand is worth two in the bush,* I think. "But you can really go for hours?" I ask him.

"With you," he answers, "I can go for days, weeks, centuries." He is really one amazing guy. I want him for a friend, a partner, an ally. I decide I will make him my guide into this brave new world of geezer love. I pull my panties and skirt all the way off and kick them across the floor.

"Get out of your pants and push that button some more," I say as I lay back on the couch, spreading my thighs.

He stands up with a wonderful smile on his face. His pants and boxers fall to his ankles. He steps out of them, kicks off the black oriental slippers he is wearing, then he takes a step toward me. His belly sags over his crotch; the extra flesh on his chest makes it look as if he has small breasts. His scrawny legs are marred with brown age spots. He puts his hand down along the side of his inner thigh and squeezes his magic button. Instantly his cock stands up, grows to twice its size. I see this pudgy old geezer coming toward me. I try to smile encouragingly, but I feel that this smile is stiff and strained. I make myself put my hands under my ass to lift my pussy up to welcome him. As he slides his astonishing cock into me, I close my eyes and try to pretend he is the great god Pan, his chubby belly holding the sex secrets of centuries.

Epilogue

I am walking down Forty-second Street a few days before Christmas, heading for the number 4 train at Grand Central. Shop windows festooned with red and green tinsel, sparkling many-colored lights shine like the gates of an earthly paradise. People surround me carrying shopping bags filled with brightly wrapped packages. Three national guardsmen lope by, carrying M16s. One of them has a Santa cap on his head. Everyone looks happy, blissed out, despite the plummeting economy, the world crisis, the impending war.

Two teen girls walking just ahead of me are wearing short, lightweight blazer jackets despite the wintry day. Chatting, laughing, and smoking cigarettes, they totter back and forth on those so-very-in-this-year pointy black stiletto heels that look like torture instruments. As I watch their graceful little ass cheeks glide up and down inside their tight jeans, I am filled with tenderness. I am wishing them the best—long nights with all-right men; plenty of good, hot mouth and hard cock—when someone falls into step beside me. I look over. It's Lionheart.

He's wearing his fine, navy cashmere coat, the one he got at Abercrombie & Fitch, but now it is stained and shabby. His hairline has receded so much he looks like former Mayor Giuliani. His face is lined, his blue eyes dull, but I know him in a second.

He moves his sorry head closer to mine.

"You were the only one, the only one who was ever true to me," he mumbles into my ear. I want to touch him, grab him, pull him close, but he turns abruptly, moves into the crowd behind me. I peer all around, but I see no trace of him. How could he have vanished so suddenly?

Stunned, I stagger into a garbage can, grab the edge to steady myself. His new old man's face flickers like a mirage before my eyes. Was this apparition real? Or does this mean Lionheart is dead and a ghost, free in his spirit form to wander? Did I create him from the lonely wasteland within me? Have I finally snapped—entered some kind of Blanche du Bois world of aging women who lose themselves in impossible dreams of lost love?

"Are you all right, dear?" My thoughts are interrupted by an elegant, ancient lady in a white mink coat. I realize I am still clutching the garbage can. "Yes, thank you, thank you," I manage to say. I pull myself together and, still shaken, continue down the block.

I pass the Krispy Kreme Doughnuts shop. In one window various doughnuts are arranged on a large tray to spell out "Peace on Earth." Blanche du Bois, I need some sweetness. I go inside and buy a doughnut, my favorite, yellow cake iced with chocolate. When the girl behind the counter hands me the doughnut in a paper wrapper, she says, "Happy holidays." I sit at a vacant table, lift the doughnut to my mouth, and stick my tongue through the hole. The chocolate melts on my tongue; it tastes like heaven. I think about where my tongue has been and where it still wants to go. I'm not

Blanche yet. I eat the donut, taking my time, down to the last crumb.

Out on the street again, I pass the Thank God It's Friday. It's so crowded, people are standing in the open door, holding their drinks. The shiny letters pasted inside the window spell out, "Merry Christmas," "Happy 2003," and "Drink Beer for a Miracle." Maybe that's the right idea.

The subway car is crowded, but there is one seat empty. I make for it and sit gratefully down. As I do, my arm pokes into the side of the person sitting next to me, an older guy wearing a black leather jacket who looks something like Yves Montand in that movie he made with Marilyn Monroe.

"Sorry, sorry," I mumble.

"That's okay," he says, grinning at me. "I don't get hit by a good-looking woman every day." He returns to his newspaper, and I try to compose myself. I try not to look over at him. I resist the temptation to put my head on his shoulder. I hope I'm not imagining it, but he seems to be pressing his thigh against mine.

I don't know where Lionheart is, but I know where I am. I am riding into the New Year on the downtown Flatbush IRT, and I am filled with rich doughnut cake, chocolate, and wonder.

the
widow

Greg Boyd

For Claire Ribbonet

The Widow*

With the sudden and unexpected death of her husband of twenty-four years, Karen Regent realized, for the first time in her life, that she was completely alone. One minute she was sailing along, humming with the radio in her car on the way home from work, wondering what to cook for dinner, and the next she was marooned on the desert island of her grief, surrounded by an ocean of despair. She'd known something was terribly wrong when she'd turned onto her street and seen the red lights of the ambulance

---

* I only recently discovered, quite by accident, that my wife was writing a pornographic novel. Of course I had no idea what it was at first. It seemed to be some kind of story about how a woman deals with her grief and loss after her husband dies suddenly. And I suppose, even now, that's still really what it's about. But I can see that I'm already getting ahead of myself. It might be better if I started at the beginning, about three weeks ago, when I first discovered a couple of pages my wife had sent from the computer to the printer and then forgot to retrieve.

flashing in her driveway. Apparently, her husband had suffered a heart attack while turning a wooden chair leg on the lathe in the garage they'd years ago converted to a shop. Though he'd managed to dial 911, the paramedics arrived too late to save him. Through her tears she kept thinking how she had meant to call him during her lunch break earlier in the day, just to say hello, but hadn't got around to it. Now a neighbor sat holding her hand while she sobbed on the couch in the living room as the paramedics wheeled his body out on a stretcher.

Throughout the funeral and afterward Karen had succumbed to a pervasive numbness, a sense of spiritual abstraction, as if she, too, had died. While she knew rationally that she still existed physically, her spirit seemed to have flown from her body, leaving her an empty husk, a shadow incapable of any real human emotion. Dressed in black, her dark and graying hair pulled severely back and clipped tightly at the nape of her neck, she'd smiled distractedly as she collected hugs and condolences from family and

---

I found them there when I went into the study to check my e-mail one evening after work. I'm a college professor, though I won't say what subject I teach, except to assure you it has nothing to do with writing, psychology, or human sexuality, and I use my e-mail frequently at home to communicate with students, colleagues, and fellow researchers from all over the world. At first I thought nothing of the papers and simply scooped them out of the tray. But when I turned them over and saw that the bottom sheet was formatted as a title page that read, "The Widow, a novel by Amanda Lighthouse," I couldn't help but examine them more closely. I mean, the whole thing was just too unlikely to ignore.

friends, while inside she throbbed with a dull ache. For a while she found it almost impossible to speak and looked longingly at others to respond on her behalf, or else simply whispered, "I'm sorry," in a voice so soft as to be almost inaudible. For days she walked around mute, her eyes blinking and squinting, her hand covering her half-open mouth.

Though her father had died when she was a teenager and she'd only recently suffered through her mother's long illness and eventual passing, the grief she felt on those occasions had been mixed with other emotions—anger, disbelief, denial—and tempered by the constant need to continue functioning, if only because she knew others (most recently her husband and her daughter) depended on her. As difficult as it had been then, the process at least seemed real to her. This time it was different. Her life now seemed to her like a bad dream from which she couldn't seem to awaken, a dream in which she found herself hopelessly lost at sea in the small, leaky vessel of her body, drifting toward a black and stormy horizon.

In retrospect, I suppose at that point I might have simply carried the pages into the next room, handed them to my wife, and said, "you left these in the printer." Then she would have told me enough about her novel to quiet my curiosity and that would have been the end of it. But I didn't, for the same reason most anyone who stumbles onto a diary can't resist sampling its contents: there's something deliciously illicit, voyeuristic, and even dangerous about the uninvited reading of someone's supposedly personal writings. Faced with such an opportunity, I found that I desperately wanted to find out for myself what she'd written.

First of all, Mandy's not, in any sense, a writer. Since she's never

With the passage of time her grief and fear of the future seemed to spread over her and solidify, sealing her off from the world around her so that even the air she breathed seemed blighted and the light of day stained and tainted. Whenever her name came up in conversation, people were apt to say something like, "Poor Karen, she's taking it awfully hard, you know."

Stumbling through a succession of days that in no way resembled her former life, one morning she found she simply lacked the will to continue. Instead of getting up, making coffee, showering, drying her hair, putting on makeup, dressing, eating her toasted bagel with cream cheese or her eggs scrambled with cheese, washing the dishes, and driving her car to her job as a grade-school teacher as she had for the past twenty-four years, she instead dozed through most of the morning. Sometime after noon she wrapped a bathrobe around herself and collapsed on the living room couch, eyes open staring blankly at the wall. Two weeks later she was on medical disability and seeing a psychologist.

---

been one to jot down her impressions, keep a record of her moods, pen long letters to friends, or even enjoy playing with words, I found her attempt at a novel rather uncharacteristic. Though she reads lots of books for pleasure, I never suspected she had any desire to write one herself. Perhaps it's something she's always secretly wanted to do. You may think you know someone pretty well after twenty years of marriage, that you have at least some kind of basic understanding of what makes that person tick, but I guess you can never be too sure.

Anyway, it also struck me as odd that she'd used her real first

After months of medication and counseling, she'd finally felt well enough to apply for a yearlong sabbatical from her job, gather up her husband's clothes and tools and donate them to the local thrift shop, and have the outside of her house painted purple and pink, colors she'd always favored but never insisted on. Then she got into her car and drove herself to California, where she planned to stay, for several months and perhaps longer, with her daughter, Melissa, her husband, Jim, a dentist, and her two young grandchildren. Melissa and Jim had a lovely large house with a red tile roof, a sand and cactus garden, and white adobe courtyard walls with arched doorways, all situated high on a hilltop overlooking a smoggy, crowded southern California valley.

Though everyone tried to make her feel welcome, as the days stretched into a week, Karen could feel that she was already intruding on carefully established patterns. While she told herself that she would be useful babysitting her grandchildren, Dotty and Paul, or else helping her daughter shop, prepare meals, and clean the house,

———————————————

name, along with an obviously humorous pseudonym. Our surname, you see, is not Lighthouse, but rather Millhouse. Was there a reason she wasn't writing under her own name?

As I looked over the opening pages of the manuscript, I detected a number of obvious similarities to the author's real life. I noted, for example, that my wife's protagonist, Karen Regent, was close to the same age as Mandy and even had her lovely chestnut hair touched with gray. More to the point, Mandy's father, too, had died when she was a teenager, and her mother had only recently passed away after a debilitating illness. And while our daughter,

she knew that she was outside the rhythm of their routine—a life of child care, mortgage payments, and careers, a life of conversations about money and the future, a life that closely resembled the one she had once shared with her husband. Because the spare bedroom was next to their own, and voices carried easily through the thin walls of the house, she knew that Melissa and Jim would have to remind each other to be quiet whenever they were intimate.

Somehow it didn't feel quite right ironing Jim's shirts and folding his stiff white underwear. And though he was almost terminally pleasant, his fine white teeth always quick to flash at her, Karen could sense that he nonetheless resented her presence in his home. She also knew that Melissa disapproved of the way she deferred to Jim like she had always deferred to her husband. For their part, Paul and Dottie followed her around the house like two puppies, crying, whining, and banging their little fists against the door whenever she tried to use the bathroom. Though it was a big house, it simply wasn't big enough.

Elizabeth, is a senior in high school and still lives at home, after years of classroom teaching, Mandy works as the vice principal of an elementary school.

Most disturbing to me, of course, was the garage that had been converted into a shop, for, as anyone who knows me well can attest, turning wooden table legs on the lathe and constructing reproductions of fine antique furniture is both my hobby and my passion. Several years ago I even constructed a cottage-style outbuilding with hand-split cedar shingle siding in our backyard to serve as my woodworking studio. Though the construction of the studio dis-

"But, Mom, you just got here," Melissa complained when Karen told her she was leaving. "Can't you stay at least another week?" But despite Melissa's heartfelt feelings and best intentions, Karen knew that even her daughter was just being polite. Though concerned for her welfare, Melissa was clearly relieved to be absolved of the responsibility of balancing the needs of her husband with those of her mother.

So after smoothing the crease on her daughter's brow and hugging and kissing each of her grandchildren, Karen got into her car once more and drove it right back where she had started. When her friends teased her over lunch for being too independent to want to live with her daughter, she shook her head and laughed along with them.

At home later she cried herself to sleep. So nothing had changed. On the surface she'd learned how to function once more, but inside there remained an immense void. Though she continued to mourn her husband, and missed his good humor and companionship

---

placed some of Mandy's roses, I had no idea she'd held such a long-standing grudge against it.

And so even though Mandy had projected a good five years or more into the future, it was easy to see that almost everything in her manuscript seemed to be based roughly on our current life. I suppose that would make her novel what the French call a "roman à clef," or a novel with a key, which is to say a work of fiction that is based closely on real people and events.

With all this in mind, I'm sure you can easily empathize with the horror with which I read of my own demise from a heart attack

each day, she also mourned the self that had disappeared, for she hardly recognized the woman with the brittle hair and red eyes who peered back at her in the mirror.

Even her body had turned against her. It felt thick, closed, sealed off, more like a hard shell than warm, living flesh. Where she had once paused to admire her figure after getting out of the shower in the morning, now she briskly dried herself and moved away to escape her reflection. A sudden memory washed over her of how she had stood before the mirror and watched through the foggy glass as her husband reached from behind to cup her large breasts, weighing them, stroking and pulling the aroused nipples between his fingers and thumbs. She shuddered to think of what it would be like now to touch the pale, cold marble of her body. Pulling the towel tightly around her, she hurried off to get dressed.

Having treated her for depression and counseled her through her grief, Karen's therapist, Dr. Knowles, next proposed travel. "Not some visit to your busy relatives," he added, "but a relaxing vaca-

---

(standing at the lathe in my own studio, no less). That she'd had her character—"the husband" we'll call him, for he's never named and appears alive only long enough to make a dying emergency phone call—dial 911, seems to comment obliquely on my unwillingness to install a phone in my studio for fear of being interrupted. But let's not allow these minor quibbles to distract us from the main point: That Mandy's novel was somehow premised on my own death completely unnerved me.

I found it almost impossible to believe that my own dear wife and companion of so many years had, as it were, killed me off, and was trying out a fictional life without me. That poor, forsaken

tion in an exotic place." He told her travel might help her revive her interest in life. "Meet some new people," he suggested, "see something different and have some new experiences. Sometimes spicy food will awaken dormant taste buds. What have you got to lose?" So, unsure of herself but habitually obedient to authority, Karen agreed to take a trip. Though Dr. Knowles preferred a cruise to Hawaii or the Bahamas, she had always wanted to visit Europe, and so she signed up for a monthlong group tour that she hoped would help give her some purpose and provide a sense of adventure.

*   *   *

For inspiration, Karen took with her an anthology of travel writings by women who had dared to explore the world at large, who had voluntarily forsaken their comfort zone and ventured into unknown realms. These women had visited lost tribes in the jungle along the Amazon River, rode horses on the steppes of Mongolia, hitchhiked alone from Istanbul to Bangkok. One of the authors was

---

Karen Regent was having such a hard time of it was of little consolation to me. After all, she'd live on in the coming pages, whereas I was gone forever, clutching my heart and rolled out in a body bag on page 1, buried, if not yet forgotten, on page 2.

When I'd finished reading those shocking opening pages for the third time, I had to stop myself from ripping them to shreds and balling my fists for an ugly confrontation. Part of me wanted to burst into the living room, where I knew I'd find Mandy watching television with the dog's head resting comfortably on her thigh, and scream, "What have you done?" But after so many years of cohabitation, the rational part of me knew such antics would lead

a grandmother like herself, while others were professional writers, college students, or simply young women in search of themselves. All had feared for their lives or their personal safety at some point in their travels. Most had met with kindness from strangers and experienced moments of profound beauty and immense personal satisfaction. One had been raped and held captive. "The truly adventurous must travel alone," Karen read sometime during the first week of her tour. By then, of course, it was too late for such advice.

From the beginning, the trip had been a mad rush of jet lag, unfamiliar food and its unfortunate intestinal consequences, unusual and sometimes unpleasant company, and constant motion. Karen and her travel companions, most of whom were retired couples older than herself, were chauffeured in an air-conditioned double-decker bus from Amsterdam, through the major cities of the Netherlands, Belgium, Germany, and Switzerland, then down to Rome, Naples, and Venice, and back up along the French Côte d'Azure. Though for the most part she felt herself out of step with

---

nowhere constructive, so I simply replaced the pages in the tray of the printer, facedown as I'd found them, and called out to my wife that I'd be in my studio if she needed me.

That night I paced within my sanctuary, alternately fuming with anger and obsessing on my body fat and cholesterol count, while quiet in its corner, the lathe seemed to mock me. I couldn't help but pity myself, for I felt seriously betrayed. Besides, there was something unnatural, something almost fiendish, about Mandy leading this fictional double life. Suddenly the reserved and rather dignified woman I married had dressed herself in gypsy garb, cut short

her fellow travelers, during the first week Karen nevertheless managed to strike up a number of useful acquaintanceships—enough to help counter the boredom of long hours of travel.

As the trip progressed and she got to know some of the others on a deeper level, Karen found herself increasingly drawn to a woman named Jana. An artist from Minnesota, Jana was several years younger than Karen and also traveling alone. Quiet, self-possessed, and pretty in an unadorned and fragile way, Jana seemed complex and intriguing, as if she'd lived a life that was completely outside of Karen's own experience. As they talked, Karen came to admire Jana's resolve, her confidence, and her independence.

"There's nothing stopping you from doing whatever you want," she told Karen. "Just create the life you envision."

"Well, it's never been easy for me," Karen said. "I learned that whatever I wanted didn't really matter in the larger scheme of things. I mean, there have always been other people to consider. In a way I suppose I used my husband and my daughter as an excuse.

---

the lifeline on my palm, and installed herself in some crystal ball future.

There's a fairy tale, I recall, about a man who marries a witch. Every day they're together he shrinks a little. At first he doesn't notice, but after a while it's obvious because his pants start to droop down over his shoes, which are now too big for him as well. Before long he's reduced to the size of a child, and still he's shrinking. Finally he starts to wise up and realizes the only way to reverse the spell and regain his former stature is to get rid of the witch. But by now he's tiny and she's more powerful than ever.

Because my life didn't allow for me to pursue my own identity, I didn't have to feel bad about not having one. Anyway, I don't think I could ever be that brave."

"Oh, Karen, of course you could. You can't expect that everything will go right all the time, but you've got to take chances. Just figure out what you want to do and go for it. What have you really got to lose?"

Over the next couple of days there were times when Karen thought she noticed Jana staring at her in a strange way. It was almost as if she was trying to memorize her features. When Karen looked back at her, Jana only smiled and kept staring until Karen lowered her eyes and busied herself with her camera. Once, Karen felt so uncomfortable with the staring that she tried to distract Jana with a question.

"Oh, heavens no," Jana had laughed when Karen asked her if she'd ever been married or had children. Though Karen didn't pry, she couldn't help from wondering.

He thinks he might be able to stick a needle in her eye when she's asleep, but there's a big cat that watches him constantly and won't let him near her. He spends most of his time locked inside a birdcage in order to keep himself safe from the damned cat. Meanwhile, the lovely girl who was once his bride but who somehow turned into an evil, demented bitch, thinks seeing him in a birdcage is about the funniest thing ever. But as bad as things look for him, in the end he gets her, though I don't remember exactly how.

I realized, of course, that I was probably overreacting and letting myself become melodramatic. But my feelings had been bruised, and I suppose at that point I was feeling pretty low and deflated,

That night, alone in her hotel room, when Karen thought about Jana, she wondered if her husband would have found her friend attractive. He'd once admitted to her that he'd always had a fantasy about being with two women at the same time. She wondered if he would have tried to imagine what Jana's thin, petite body looked like under her clothes. Would he have wanted to unbraid her straight brown hair so that it fell over her shoulders? Would he have caressed her neck and kissed her soft lips? Or would he have preferred instead to watch his wife kiss Jana, as her fingers worked at the buttons of her friend's blouse, revealing the small, pointed breasts? Would he have then ordered her to touch her friend's wet vagina, to pleasure another woman with her lips and tongue, to sample the tide of her excitment as he, in turn, thrust his erection into Jana's mouth, watching them both, like some high priest enacting an ancient fertility rite?

A few days later when the two women were sitting side by side on the bus, Jana said to Karen, "I have a favor to ask of you, but please

———————————————

like a balloon or a tire that someone had let the air out of. So maybe it wasn't too much of a stretch to compare myself to that poor, shrinking husband and Mandy to the witch. At any rate, I told myself that, since I'd inadvertently exposed my wife's secret life, it was in my best interest to find out exactly where it was going.

So the next day, and each day thereafter, I looked for further installments of that damned story. Of course by then Mandy had retrieved her hard copy from the tray on the printer. But it was easy enough to search the hard drive on the computer for her recent work. Sure enough, there was a file called "Widow" among her most recent documents. From the date stamping on

realize that you don't have to agree to it." For a moment Karen was unable to answer. She felt a blush of desire and fear sweep over her in a wave as she remembered her fantasy. The blood pounded in her temples.

"You have a wonderful face, Karen," Jana said, "so soft and pretty." By now Karen was twisting slightly in her seat, flustered and embarrassed by her own imagination, as well as by the implications of the compliment. She felt her blush deepen. "I'd like to draw you, if you wouldn't mind."

Karen shook her head and turned quickly away. "No, of course not."

"Just relax then and face forward," Jana told her, as she removed a pad of paper and a box of pencils from the case she had stowed under her seat. Then she reached over and gently tucked a strand of Karen's hair back behind her ear. The artist's fingers lingered for a moment, warm on Karen's cheek. "That's better," she said. Karen breathed as deeply as she could manage, her heart beating quickly

------

the revision log I could see that she usually wrote for about an hour at a stretch on days she got home early from work. As soon as Mandy went to bed that night I went to the computer and opened her file.

Over the course of the next week I learned how Karen had gone slightly bonkers after my funeral, but in time medicated herself back into working order. Evidently, however, she was still damaged goods, as she failed to make a connection with her daughter's life in California, frequently cried herself to sleep, and let herself be bullied by her therapist into foreign travel as a means of, in Dr. Feelgood's words, "reviving her interest in life." Well, well.

as she listened to the sound of the pencils scratching beside her. When she'd finished, Jana tore the paper from the pad and handed it to Karen. The drawing was inscribed, "To lovely Karen, almost ready to fly," and signed, "Jana D."

Despite her degree in liberal studies and her background as a teacher who had always prided herself on making history and art come alive for her pupils, initially Karen had a difficult time with the pace of the tour. She grew so annoyed with being ushered from one masterpiece to the next that she often opted to take a walk by herself during the allotted half-hour stops at museums. When the tour visited a cathedral, she left the others to the chattering guide and sat in the darkest corner concentrating her attention on a single stained-glass window. Too much history and too many countries left her cranky and overstimulated.

When, after two weeks of travel, the bus finally rolled into Italy, Karen began to take a more active interest in her surroundings. Instead of playing card games, reading whatever English language

---

I wondered why Mandy had sent her alter ego to Europe when the two of us had spent so many great summer vacations together in southern France. For a while we'd even fantasized about buying an old house in some lost village and living there after we both retired. Couldn't she leave well enough alone? Why did Karen Regent now have to soil everything with her greedy revisionism? Why couldn't she instead head off to India to seek enlightenment, or Jamaica to experience ganja bliss?

Aside from the jealousy and anger the manuscript inspired in me, I disliked my wife's literary debut for other, more technical reasons as well. Frankly, "The Widow" was starting to get boring. The

newspaper could be found, complaining about the food, or talking about how much better things were at home like most of the other travelers, she often found herself staring out the window of the bus as it passed through unnamed villages. She wondered about the lives people lived behind the thick stone walls of the houses and imagined herself walking along those same streets, learning to speak the language, slowly finding her way.

Though uninspired by the dank churches and polluted water-ways of Venice and overwhelmed by the endless parade of high art and the constant display of wealth and religious relics at the Vatican, Karen was drawn to the practical marvels of the ancient Romans, their aqueducts, roads, temples, and arenas. A direct and often brutal people, the Romans offered their enemies a choice between assimilation and enslavement. Seeing physical evidence of their accomplishments inspired in Karen admiration for the force, ingenuity, and vitality of their civilization.

One day, when the tour stopped for lunch at a village restaurant

---

descriptions of European settings were strangely flat, and even Karen seemed less than fully fleshed out. I mean, nobody could be quite that helpless and lost. And seriously, how many ugly Americans does it take to fill a tour bus? While the lesbian intrigue with Jana did temporarily revive my interest (after all, what man hasn't at one time or another entertained such fantasies?), in general, the story seemed flat and unrealistic. One thing was certain: Mandy had no future as a novelist.

I'd also have to say that I was a little disappointed in my wife for writing what I felt was so obviously the literary equivalent of a "chick flick," which is to say a narrative in which a weak, overly de-

with outdoor tables, she gave away a small fortune to a little boy in dirty clothes who came peddling flowers. "You shouldn't encourage them, you know," a man from her group scolded from the next table. She watched the wrinkles in his neck wiggle as he talked. "The guide said not to give them money."

* * *

Four days later, when the bus left Nice for Paris and the flight home, Karen was not on it. The tour manager warned her sternly that she would forfeit her return plane ticket if she missed the scheduled flight. "It's okay," she apologized. "It doesn't matter if I go home. I'm a widow." The tour representative twisted his mustache and bowed slightly, his expression betraying nothing.

Though far from leaving her wealthy, her late husband's life insurance, along with their combined savings accounts, property investments, municipal bonds, and retirement accounts, as well as the fact that they'd already paid off the twenty-year mortgage on

---

pendent middle-aged woman sets out in search of herself and ends up conquering her fears and the world with the help of the amazing women she meets along the way. Sisterhood to the rescue and all that rot. It was just so damned predictable.

So I was fast losing interest in the manuscript and had almost forgiven Mandy for killing me off, as doing so had at least saved me from the horrible fate of being a character in a bad novel. Furthermore, I'd only just been selected to serve on the hiring committee within the department and had been so busy looking over the applications of prospective new hires that I let nearly a week go by without checking the computer for an updated version of "The

their house, meant that, if she lived modestly, she could probably afford to spend the rest of the decade, if not the rest of her life, without much concern for money. It was the first time she had given her finances solid consideration, and she found the thought of her independence almost intoxicating.

As the bus pulled away, Karen waved good-bye from the palm-lined sidewalk in front of the hotel. She'd liked Jana well enough, and had even exchanged phone numbers, addresses, and a hug with her, but she was glad to see the others go. As soon as the bus was out of sight, Karen consulted her phrase book and hired a cab. "*Un hôtel près de la plage? S'il vous plait?*" The driver nodded. He put her suitcase in the trunk, tugged at the waist of his sagging pants, and adjusted his cap.

"To the beach," he said, smiling over his cigarette and exposing a row of chipped brown teeth. After finding a room in an hotel a block from the main promenade and waiting almost two hours in a café for a bowl of onion soup served by a waiter in a stiff white

---

Widow." I'm not sure why I even came back to it, but I did. And suddenly everything changed.

Free at last from the confining influences and attitudes of her unwelcome companions on the tour bus, Karen decides to hit the beach on the French Riviera, where she discovers that European women often sunbathe topless. Ooo-la-la. She buys herself a black bikini and takes it back to her hotel room for a solo fashion show. At this point I'm no longer bored with the plot. And then, suddenly, dramatically, and with great flair, I'm back from the dead, caressing her naked breasts, if only in her memory.

And just to set the record straight, it's true that I love Mandy's

apron, Karen walked to the beach, where she saw a jumble of bronzed bodies glistening under colorful umbrellas. The brilliant afternoon sky ate up any trace of shadow, giving the bodies, the buildings behind them, and even the sea itself a flat and powerful aspect. The whole world seemed charged with the raw and primal energy of the sun.

Karen noted that many of the women on the beach were topless, their breasts exposed to the sunlight and to the gaze of others nearby. Sitting on the sand in her white shorts and T-shirt, her sunglasses and a red bandanna tied over her hair, she felt the sun kiss the uncovered skin of her forearms, calves, and knees, and she craved more. As she watched a young couple splashing together at the shoreline, she thought of running naked toward the cool, inviting water and diving in.

The next morning she went shopping for a bathing suit. She found a small boutique along the promenade, where a serious young salesgirl fitted her into a black bikini with a shelflike bra that

---

breasts, that when we were younger I could hardly constrain myself from touching them in public, that it delights me to this day to take her thick brown nipples between my lips and gently suck and bite them, to lap at them with my tongue.

And so I found the image of my wife, or rather her fictional alter ego, standing before the mirror in a hotel room in Nice, dressed in black panties and caressing her naked breasts, lovely and stirring, as if I'd caught a glimpse of some private moment through a crack in the bathroom door. When the author invited me to stay and watch Karen shave her thighs and trim her pubic hair, I was only too eager to accept.

pushed her breasts together, creating a generous expanse of cleavage. "*Ça vous allez très bien, Madame,*" the clerk commented. "*Vous permettez?*" she asked, reaching to adjust the cups of the bra slightly. "*Oui, c'est parfait.*" She nodded her solemn approval. After changing back into her dress, Karen handed over a wad of crumpled bills, from which the girl made change.

"*Merci, Mademoiselle,*" Karen said.

"*Au revoir, Madame.*" A little bell clanged as the door shut behind her.

Filled with confidence, Karen bought herself a wide-brimmed straw hat in another store and stopped to marvel at the display of beautiful lace lingerie in the window of a boutique around the corner from her hotel.

Back in her room she tried on the black two-piece swimsuit and looked at herself in the mirror. She noted critically that her behind had spread with age and become a bit flabby, though her long legs were still well shaped. Her bust had always been well endowed,

---

What happened next shocked and excited me, for I'd never seen Mandy masturbate nor even heard her discuss it. I knew she'd probably done it in the past, probably did it even now, discreetly in bed beneath the covers when I was out of town or in the bath perhaps when she needed to unwind after a long week at work. Thinking about it sent blood racing to my penis. I couldn't believe, however, that she'd set down in writing a detailed description of such an intimate and personal act. As I mentioned, seeing her with the razor had already given me an erection. But when I read how she brazenly watched her own fingers spread herself open in the re-

though over the years her shoulders had become rounded and her breasts sagged considerably. But the bikini top thrust them up and made her look attractive, almost sexy. She imagined the dark foreign men on the beach looking at her. Not too bad for an old lady, they'd say to themselves.

She unpinned her long hair and shook it loose. Dark and streaked throughout with gray, her hair was thick, wavy, and natural. Then she reached behind her, unhooked the bikini top, and tossed it onto the bed behind her. She watched herself in the mirror as she weighed her heavy breasts in her hands. Her husband had loved them. She remembered how he used to pinch, pull, and suck on her erect nipples whenever they made love. She closed her eyes and brushed her fingers in circles around their tips, feeling them harden with her touch.

Karen moaned out loud and caught herself. Opening her eyes she saw herself standing half naked in the mirror. Patches of dark hair protruded from either side of the black bikini bottom. *I'll have*

---

flection of the mirror, I couldn't help from touching myself through my trousers.

Of course Mandy would never give voice to a word like *cunt*. She was far too proper, too much the lady, ever to indulge in dirty talk. Even the occasional moan that escaped her during our lovemaking tended to be subdued, for she was always conscious of our daughter's presence in the house. At rare moments when my passion overcame me, she gently reminded me with a whisper that we must be quiet for Elizabeth's sake. "It wouldn't be fair to her," she reasoned.

to shave that, she thought, and headed for the bathroom. Slipping the bottoms down to her ankles, she stepped out of them as she ran warm water in the sink before her. She set one foot up on the edge of the sink, splashed water onto her thighs, and rubbed a bar of soap onto the hair. She carefully ran her razor along the sensitive skin of her inner thigh, starting from the V of her crotch. When she finished shaving her thighs and legs, she thinned the pubic hair around her sex and shaved it well below the bikini line on top. Then she splashed water all over her mound and patted herself dry with a towel.

Quickly she thought to pluck her eyebrows and searched her luggage for her handheld magnifying mirror and a pair of tweezers. She sat down on the edge of the bed and stared at her enlarged eyes reflected in the glass. At first the pain of pulling the tiny hairs out by their roots distracted her from the tingling sensation that lingered between her thighs. But in the end she found she simply couldn't ignore it, so she carefully set the tweezers down on the nightstand.

As for Beth, I was convinced she knew a great deal more about carnal pleasure than her mother ever suspected. Late one Friday night several months earlier, when I'd got up from bed and stumbled to the kitchen for a glass of water, I'd seen her on the floor of the darkened living room with her legs wrapped around her boyfriend's thrusting buttocks. His pants were bunched around his ankles and her skirt gathered at her waist. Evidently, she'd inherited or learned to imitate her mother's capacity for silent and secretive fucking. Not wanting to cause a scene or embarrass them, I'd gone back to bed with my heart pounding and my throat parched.

Unlike her whispered obscenities, Karen's admission that sex

She sighed and felt herself blush as she spread her legs wide and lowered the mirror until it rested between them, reflecting now the secret folds of her vagina. She used the fingers of her free hand to gently spread the outer lips, exposing the glistening opening, then pulled the fleshy hood up over the shiny pebble of her clitoris and sighed again. "Cunt," she whispered.

The sound of the word excited her. She'd never said it out loud before. In fact, she'd never really examined herself closely down there before either. She wasn't that kind of woman, as she liked to remind herself. But by now she was wet and agitated, and if a word, an image, a magnified view of her own genitals could bring her pleasure, then why should she deny herself? After all, she was alone, completely alone. As she slid a finger along the slippery crease, she didn't know whether to grit her teeth or smile. Instead she breathed out heavily, a rush of air passing through her pursed lips.

It had been a long time since she'd touched herself and she couldn't even remember when she'd last had an orgasm. Somehow

---

had become increasingly less important to her, that she depended on her husband to take the lead in their love life, and that she rarely reached a climax, all had the dull ring of truth. And though I found these admissions worrisome and slightly deflating, I nonetheless skipped over them for the moment, for I could tell something good was pending in the narrative. Okay, I'll admit that I had already unzipped my fly and taken my penis in hand and it was too late for rational discourse. By now it seemed only right that I should finish what she'd started.

It was the mirror that did it for me. Watching my mate insert into her spread-open *cunt* the pink plastic handle of the vanity

such things had became less important to her over the years. In her marriage she'd let her husband take the lead where sex was concerned, and though she almost never had an orgasm during their lovemaking, she never liked to call attention to herself or discuss her sexuality, which embarrassed her. So if she was missing something, she didn't mind at all. It certainly wasn't worth all the fuss and worry, and she really did enjoy giving her husband pleasure. As for masturbation, she'd always thought there was something selfish and narcissistic about the process, and even though it was a private affair, she usually couldn't get past her embarrassment and take it seriously enough to get aroused.

Maybe it was the raw and naked sunlight, the way the bodies glistened with sweat and oil on the beach that coaxed her desire, but Karen felt an impossible to ignore need to bring herself to a climax. She shuddered as she thrust a finger into her wetness and stirred it around inside. Slowly she pushed another finger in and then pulled both of them out and rubbed small circles around her

---

mirror I'd seen each day for years on top of her dresser was more than I could take. My semen shot up over my fingers and onto the keyboard. It amazed me that she'd taken a common object from our life together and infused it with such eroticism: Looking at that fictional yet still very real mirror was like viewing a reflection of my deepest fantasies, my most primitive and raw desires.

Overcome with guilty pleasure, and wet with my own ejaculate, I cleaned up as best I could, using a monogrammed handkerchief Mandy had given me for Christmas.

Part of me wanted to go directly to our bedroom, wake Mandy up, and plead with her to masturbate in front of me, with the light

protruding clit. She licked her lips and brought her fingers to them and tasted the musky scent. For a moment she thought about Jana, how soft her hand had felt against her cheek, how her hand had lingered a second too long. As she stared into the magnified reflection of her ripe vagina, she allowed herself to imagine what it might be like to lie entwined in the soft embrace of another woman, to touch and taste *cunt*. That word again. She shook at the thought, rubbing her clit frantically. It was going to happen. She was almost there when her leg started to cramp from the awkward position, stopping her just short of her orgasm.

Suddenly her eye fell upon the long plastic handle of her mirror and she stood up and squeezed her legs together against her hand. Still holding the mirror, she flopped down onto the bed, lying on her back with her legs drawn up toward her chest. Though she'd never penetrated herself with an object before during masturbation, she didn't hesitate now. "The truly adventurous travel alone," she reminded herself as she grabbed the mirror by the rounded

———————————

on and the curtains open, to *suck my cock* until I geysered sperm all over her belly, her breasts, her lovely face. I wanted to slap my penis against her cheek and tell her how much I loved to watch my erection slide between her lips. Instead, I reread the section in which Karen dismisses her sexual desires as "not worth all the fuss and worry." I couldn't help from feeling enormously guilty and inadequate. All of this was so terribly confusing.

I realized that over the years I'd become a lazy and predictable lover, that I'd somehow lost touch with both her fantasies and my own. Though we'd once been as hot to rut as any young couple, somehow over time sex had become a topic that was practically off

glass end and slowly inserted the handle inside. Then she bucked her pelvis and rolled her hips, fucking herself. "Oh fuck me, fuck me, fuck me," she chanted, her inhibitions temporarily on vacation, her embarrassment forfeited to her pleasure. When she felt herself ready to come, she pulled the handle out and, spreading the folds of her labia to fully expose her clitoris, rubbed the slick plastic briskly against it until she cried out and collapsed, shaking in the middle of the bed.

Later, of course, she luxuriated in her guilt. First, she took a nap, then had a cool drink in the downstairs café, where she passed the rest of the afternoon reading a paperback novel. *The beach could wait another day,* she thought as she watched the people who walked along the sidewalk and passed by her shady table. Pedestrian traffic had begun to thin out with the early evening, as tourists and vacationers made their way back to their hotels to change clothes for dinner. She had just decided to leave the café herself and look for a place to buy a sandwich that she could eat in

limits. Our sexual pleasure, real or imagined, was something we simply didn't discuss. And yet clearly Mandy had an erotic impulse that was as unsatisfied, repressed, and frustrated as my own. Her fantasy life was a side of her I knew nothing about, a part of her I had lost.

Mandy and I desperately needed to talk. I resolved to set aside the time for it the very next day, which happened to be a Friday. A romantic dinner out after work would help facilitate the conversation. Later, after a few drinks, some candid discussion, and a mutual promise never to let ourselves become so estranged again, we'd make love with a complete lack of inhibition. I'd get us a room in a

her room, when a well-dressed stranger approached her table and began addressing her in French. Thin and dark-haired, with sharp, handsome features, he stared intently into her eyes as he spoke. She estimated his age somewhere in the range of thirty-five to forty. After several sentences, accompanied by hand gestures, it finally became clear to him the she did not understand a word he was saying.

"I'm sorry," he said, in heavily accented English. "Excuse me. I did not realize you were not French. You are English?"

"American," Karen responded.

"Wonderful. I mistook you for one of our film stars. So silly. Now I'm very much embarrassed." He shook his hand limply from side to side. "I was going to ask for your autograph. Can you believe it?" He laughed at himself and smiled warmly. "But let me introduce myself anyway," he continued. "My name is Alain. Alain Mercure."

"Karen Regent," she said, offering her hand.

---

hotel if need be. I was thinking about reservations when I suddenly remembered that I'd already agreed to attend a retirement party that night for a professor of philosophy I barely knew. The dean had mentioned that he'd see me there, so it was impossible to cancel. Worse, I was leaving the morning after for a weekend faculty retreat. I let my face collapse into my open palms and sighed aloud, as I imagined Mandy sitting at the keyboard, her libido unleashed, doing God knows what in my absence.

The entire weekend of the retreat I felt distracted and out of place. I found it difficult to concentrate on the discussions relating to university policy and curriculum development. Even my presen-

Taking it between his own, he lifted her fingers slowly to his lips. "*Enchanté, Madame.*" After a long moment he released her hand and slid into the chair next to her. "You don't mind?" he waved, taking a cigarette from the pocket of his jacket. Startled, Karen shook her head. "Good, then tell me, please, what a beautiful woman like you is doing sitting all afternoon by herself in a café?"

For a moment Karen's face went rigid and white as the thought occurred to her that he'd been watching her from a distance for hours and that she'd been singled out for some kind of con. All her life she'd been cautious and mistrustful of strangers. She told herself that she should get up and leave the café, leave this man immediately, but somehow her limbs refused to obey. Around her she felt the soothing hum of conversation, and when she looked up, she saw that Alain was gently stroking her palm with his thumb and smiling brightly as he related an anecdote about an encounter between one of his business associates' elderly uncle, a country farmer, and a carload of German tourists. He waved the stub of his

---

tation concerning the candidates for the open faculty position, which I'd prepared so carefully, came across as flat and uninspired, my recommendations safe and predictable. Several of my colleagues commented that I didn't look well, that my color was off. I'd been suffering from migraines, I explained. In truth, however, I couldn't stop thinking of Mandy.

More than anything I wanted to tell her how I worshipped the violin curve of her hips and breasts, the soft flesh of her neck and inner thighs, the smell of her hair. I wanted to touch her and kiss her and hold her naked body under the starlit sky. I wanted her to burn her stupid novel and come back to me.

cigarette and crushed it out in the plastic ashtray on the table for emphasis, laughing deeply. His dark eyes sparkled.

Meanwhile, a carafe of wine and two glasses had appeared on the table, and Karen found herself drinking a toast to good health and happiness. Fifteen minutes later she had agreed to have dinner with Alain, who insisted she accompany him to a little-known restaurant—a jewel in the rough, he said—on the outskirts of town. "You'd never find it on your own," he told her, "and I assure you it's not to be missed."

The restaurant was on the ground floor of a tiny inn, a three-story stone building at the intersection of two country roads. There were six tables inside and three more set within a garden patio directly alongside the road. To take advantage of the pleasant weather, Alain suggested they eat outside. "It's noisy here with the cars, but the outdoors is good for the appetite." He shrugged his shoulders. "You can't win."

Both restaurant and hotel were operated by an enormously fat

I knew I'd lost her the minute I got home. Dressed in a chic black turtleneck and corduroy pants, she was sitting at the kitchen table eating a croissant and drinking espresso. Her hair looked shiny and her face seemed to glow from within.

I learned later that his name was Alain and that he was a photographer. They'd met in a café when he claimed to have mistaken Karen for a French film star, or at least that's the line he fed her. Though she didn't quite buy it, he managed to charm her nonetheless. Tall, dark, handsome, charming, sophisticated, and French, he was probably everything my wife would have dreamed of in a fantasy man. In addition, he was a good ten years younger than me.

man and his thin wife, who came to the table to shake hands and introduce themselves. The man did the cooking, he explained, and his wife served. "If you don't eat well," the cook boasted, "you don't have to pay."

"Never trust a thin cook," said Alain when they were alone again.

Over dinner he told Karen that he was a photographer. "I mostly take pictures of people. You know, weddings and portraits of children. Sometimes I work with video as well. I do what I can to keep busy." When he asked about Karen's life, she candidly told him whatever he wanted to know, how she'd married right after college, raised a family, worked as a teacher, how she came to be in France, alone. He was a good listener and asked thoughtful, probing questions. In response, he gave up very little. "I grew up here," he told her at one point, his hand making a big circle over his head. "I know my way around."

As promised, the food was excellent: light to match the hot weather, yet full of the rich tastes of the region. "Did you like it, or

---

And yes, Mandy went to some length, if you'll excuse the pun, to describe his uncircumcised penis in a way that made it all too obvious that it was bigger than mine.

But I'm getting ahead of myself again. When I got home from the faculty retreat and found Mandy sitting at the kitchen table, I immediately told her how much I'd missed her and then bent down to give her a kiss. Instead of just an affectionate peck on the lips, however, I pushed my tongue deep inside her mouth. Neither of us wanted to break the kiss, so she wrapped her arms around my neck and pulled me closer as I touched her breast through the fabric of

should I pay just for myself?" Alain joked over coffee. Karen laughed and touched his hand. After the drive back to town, they walked along the promenade that overlooked the Mediterranean and made plans to meet at the beach the next day. Finally, Alain escorted her back to her hotel. "Good night, *chérie,*" he said, kissing her fingers once more.

In bed that night Karen wondered if she shouldn't get up, pack her suitcase, and go directly to the train station. By noon she could be in Paris and the next day on a flight home. Though she was attracted to Alain, it was a dangerous flirtation, for there was something she didn't quite trust about him. But with the thought of home came a reminder, like a sudden wave of nausea, of the awful emptiness of the past months. She remembered what Jana had told her: "You've got to create the life you want. . . . Just figure out what you want to do and go for it. . . ."

The next morning, after coffee and croissants at the hotel, Karen bought a straw beach mat and some sunscreen lotion and headed

---

her sweater and bra. Then I moved my lips to her ear and neck, kissing, nibbling, and sucking until she moaned out loud. Soon we were in the bedroom, the door locked behind us, our clothes in heaps on the floor and our bodies locked together in a savage embrace.

I was surprised at how aggressively Mandy pursued her own pleasure, mounting me as soon as I was fully erect and riding me to a quick and violent orgasm. The way she moved, the noises she made, and the force and urgency of her climax all seemed different to me and very exciting. It was as though she'd been exposed to

for the shoreline. She was wearing sandals, her new straw hat and sunglasses, and carrying a large canvas sack that contained her purse, a paperback novel, and her passport. Over the black bikini she had on a long skirt and a short-sleeved navy T-shirt. Alain was waiting for her on the boardwalk above the beach where they had arranged to meet. He seemed taller than she remembered, and it was difficult to recognize him behind his dark glasses. "Ah Karen, there you are," he said when he saw her. He leaned forward and kissed one cheek and then the other.

As they walked toward the ocean he told her he would need to be careful. "It's been a while since I've been in the sun. Except for swimming, I'll have to cover up or put some lotion on."

"I brought some sunscreen," Karen said, digging into her bag for the tube.

"Ah yes, good."

They found a spot near the water and unrolled their mats. Alain unbuttoned his shirt and slipped it off, revealing a broad, hairy

---

some new techniques and adopted an attitude of sensual fulfillment in my absence, both of which combined to result in the best sex we'd had in years.

Afterward, we talked and joked with each other the way we used to. The pure force of our physical intimacy had drawn us back together again, and I felt restored and complete for the first time in a long while. As I relaxed that evening I told myself there would be plenty of opportunities in the future to work out any problems we were having together. For the moment I couldn't bear to ruin such a wonderful evening by asking Mandy about "The Widow."

Despite, and perhaps even because of, our successful erotic en-

chest and a flat stomach. He kicked off his sandals and pulled his shorts down his long legs. He was wearing tiny red swim trunks. "Better give me that lotion," he said. Karen watched him rub the white cream vigorously onto his arms, neck, chest, and legs. He moved with a quick, aggressive sureness. She liked watching him. When Alain had finished applying the lotion to his legs, Karen slipped her shirt quickly over her head, stood up, unzipped her skirt, and let it drop around her ankles. She felt the weight of her breasts strain against her top as she bent forward to pick up the skirt. She wondered if Alain's eyes were drawn to her cleavage.

She sat back down on her mat and folded her skirt beside her. Then she took a deep breath and turned to Alain. "You'll need some on your back," she said, taking the tube of sunscreen from him. She squeezed some onto the back of his shoulders and began rubbing it into the skin. It felt oddly electric to touch a stranger in this way. When she'd finished applying the lotion to Alain's back and to her own arms, legs, shoulders, neck, chest, and stomach, she handed

---

counter of the evening before, the next day I was again plagued by strange and complex doubts. Mandy's lovemaking had been so un-characteristically passionate and uninhibited that I couldn't help from entertaining suspicions about her novel. I could feel in my heart that something was going on that I needed to get to the bottom of. After I finished teaching my morning classes, I left a note on my office door canceling my office hours and told the department secretary I was leaving early. I mumbled something about a migraine and asked that she put a cancellation notice on the door of my afternoon class.

Then I rushed home, powered up the computer and opened

the tube back to him and said, "You'd better put some on my back, as well, if you don't mind."

"Yes, of course," he told her. "Why don't you lie down first." Karen settled herself on her stomach, took another deep breath, and waited. Suddenly she felt his fingers unhook the strap of her bikini. She rose up slightly and turned toward him. "You don't want to have lines, do you?" he said, smiling as he worked the lotion into her skin, massaging deeply around her shoulder blades. She felt herself relax as he gently slid the straps down her arms. He leaned forward and whispered, "French women don't wear bras on the beach." She closed her eyes as his fingers slid along her sides, tickling her ribs.

After he'd rubbed lotion onto the backs of her thighs and calves, Alain called out, "Let's go swim," and slapped her playfully on the buttocks. Karen rose up in surprise and crossed her arms over her swaying breasts. Alain laughed. "I startled you?"

"Yes . . . I'm afraid so." She leaned forward to retrieve her top.

———————————————

"The Widow." I had left Karen several days ago sitting in a café, reading a paperback novel. Suddenly a stranger appeared at her table, speaking French and gesturing. It was Alain, whom I think I've already mentioned, pretending to mistake her for a film star. In a country where women remain sexy well into late middle age, he was masterfully playing upon both her uncertain vanity and her heightened sense of wonder, as though the ordinary had quite suddenly and unexpectedly transformed itself into the fantastic. Sitting in the deepening afternoon shadows at an outdoor table of a café in Nice, her eyes obscured by her dark sunglasses, she believed for a moment that she had actually been mistaken for a French ac-

"You don't need that," said Alain, still chuckling. "You have beautiful tits. You should show them off like the rest of the women do."

"I'm too old for that," said Karen, blushing.

"Nonsense, you're a beautiful woman. A very beautiful woman." He slipped his arm around her, pulled her toward him, and kissed her. For a second Karen felt herself falling, as if in a dream. Then she lifted her arms and embraced him around the neck, her naked breasts pressing against his hairy chest. She closed her eyes and responded to his kiss, pushing her own tongue forcefully into his mouth. Still kissing, they lay down together side by side. His hands moved to her breasts, and she could feel his erection pressing against her thighs. Finally he broke the kiss. "We'd better cool off in the water," he said.

Hand in hand they waded into the warm Mediterranean. When the water reached their shoulders, Alain grabbed Karen from behind and began caressing her again. He slipped a hand down the

---

tress, proof positive that in this thrilling and dangerous new world of hers, anything was possible.

So Alain had disarmed and then charmed her. He sat down uninvited at her table, and within minutes they were drinking wine together and laughing like old friends. Then he insisted on escorting her to a gem of a little restaurant he was certain she'd enjoy— one she'd never find on her own. During dinner Karen had told him her personal history and explained how she had come to find herself, a well-preserved woman of a certain age, alone in southern France. Afterward, when they made plans to meet at the beach the next day, there was little doubt that she'd freely given a total

backside of her bikini bottom and felt her naked ass. He licked the salt off her neck and nibbled her earlobe. "I want to make love to you," he whispered. Karen turned to face him, and they kissed. His hand groped between her legs. She shuddered and pushed her pelvis hard against him, rubbing herself like a cat against him under the water. She felt his fingers pushing aside the cloth of her bathing suit. She moaned and closed her eyes as he pushed a finger inside her.

Suddenly a group of vacationers splashed toward them. "We'd better go somewhere more private," she said, catching his hand. "Let's go to my hotel room." Laughing like school children, they splashed together toward the beach. When they arrived at their mats, Karen reached for her towel only to discover that the bag with her purse and her passport was missing.

"Oh, shit," she said, "my wallet, my passport, everything's gone."

"Don't worry," Alain told her. He quickly began asking others around them on the beach if they'd seen anyone pass nearby.

---

stranger everything he needed to seduce her—including her implied permission. He was completely aware that she was alone and vulnerable, while she must have strongly suspected he would try to take advantage of this knowledge. And so the stage was set.

The next day the two new friends spent a lot of time rubbing suntan lotion on each other. The Frenchman even boldly unhooked the top of her bikini, telling her first that she wouldn't want to have tan lines, and then challenging her with the comment that French women weren't ashamed to show off their breasts on the beach. Eventually he succeeded in kissing her and dragging her

"Yes, I think so, monsieur," a teenage girl told him. "Only a minute or two ago a man in white shorts and shirt came walking through here very close to your mats. He headed that way, up the beach," she pointed. "I think that's him over there." Alain looked a hundred yards up the beach in the direction the girl was pointing.

"He's looking back this way right now, watching us. I'm going after him." Alain took off at a jog. Down the beach the man in white took off running as well. *"Voleur!"* Alain called out. "Don't worry, I'll get him," he called back over his shoulder.

Twenty minutes later Alain returned, the canvas bag slung over his shoulder. *"Sale Arabe,"* he said, by way of explanation. "I chased him for a long time and when I got close he threw the bag down and kept running. Of course I stopped for it. How was I to know he'd already taken the passport and money out? But at least he left the traveler's checks, which are no good to him anyway, eh?" He handed the bag to Karen. "I'm sorry."

---

topless into the ocean, where the two of them groped each other like teenagers under the warm water.

While the beach blanket romance smacked of innocence gone awry, like some twisted parody of a high school party from an earlier, more innocent age, I had to admit that the theft of Karen's passport was a subtle and effective symbol. Once her former identity—as a mother, a wife, a teacher—had been removed, Karen was completely free to pursue her fantasies without fear, guilt, or remorse. No longer psychologically restricted by the demands of her former self, she could allow her libido to travel past previously

"It's okay. It was only a couple thousand francs in cash. But the passport is a different matter. That's going to cause problems. But thank you, Alain, for going after him." She leaned forward and kissed him on the cheek.

"*C'est normal,*" Alain said, shrugging his shoulders. "I'm sorry about the money. The passport means nothing until you want to leave the country. Don't worry about a thing. I'll take you to the embassy myself when the time comes. Everything will be fine. You'll see. I'll take care of you."

"I appreciate your offer, Alain. Thank you. Right now I need a shower. Why don't you come to the hotel with me? We can have dinner together later, if you have time." On the way they stopped at a bank where Karen cashed several hundred dollars' worth of traveler's checks. "I detest money," she told Alain, "it makes people behave so poorly."

When they got to her room, Karen immediately went into the bathroom and turned on the shower. "I'll just be a minute," she

_____

established boundaries and to venture into new and exotic territory.

And so, no surprise to anyone, Karen got herself royally fucked on the bathroom floor of her hotel room. First, however, my faithless wife arranged for her lover's uncut penis to appear at eye level, so she could inspect and describe it with great care and attention to detail. When she announced with a kind of giddy glee that she'd never seen one so big, I could feel my scrotum tighten and my own member shrink farther into embarrassed hiding. Since she next compared the head of Alain's penis to an exotic pink fruit, it seemed only natural that her alter ego would want to put it in her mouth.

called out. She was rinsing the shampoo from her hair when Alain stepped into the shower and embraced her from behind. He kissed her neck as he rubbed her breasts.

"You've made me so horny, I'm going to fuck you like a bull," he breathed into her ear. Karen felt him thrust his hard penis against her ass. She turned and kissed him on the mouth, then grabbed him around the waist and lowered herself so that she was squatting before him, her mouth directly in line with his erection. The water from the shower splashed off his chest and rained down onto her face as she grasped his penis in her hand. She'd never seen an uncircumcised one up close before, and never one as big as Alain's. Tentatively she pulled the foreskin back, revealing a smooth, flared bulb like some exotic pink fruit.

"It's so big," she said, stroking it, "so beautiful."

"Put it in your mouth, Karen. Suck on it." She ran her tongue around the head, then pressed her lips along the entire length, tasting. She stroked the shaft with her hand and shook the head against

---

Of course I found this blossoming infatuation, this unwholesome imaginary affair, troubling and disconcerting, if not entirely unexpected. It was a confusing situation, to say the least, for I admit that it both shamed and excited me to read her depictions of sex with another man. For me then to say that I was angry with and resentful of my wife for creating a fictional character who cheated on her dead husband seemed absurd. In the end I consoled myself with the fact that Mandy's little fictional fling meant nothing next to the fleshy excesses we had enjoyed together the night before. For, despite all his cocksure bravado, Alain could only rut with Karen like a paper bull between the sheets of an unpublished manuscript,

her closed lips, teasing him. Finally she slipped it inside her mouth. He moaned as she drew him deeper. She'd almost forgotten what it was like—the thick, warm flesh filling her mouth. Holding the base in her hand, she moved her head up and down his erection, creating suction with her lips.

"Oh yes, Karen, I can see that you know just how to do it," Alain said, his voice husky with lust. "You like to suck cock, don't you?" When Karen moaned without stopping, he pushed himself farther into her throat. "Take it all, my slut, my beautiful cocksucker." His words both shocked and excited her, and not knowing quite how to respond, she closed her eyes and swallowed him as deeply as she could take him. Suddenly he grabbed the back of her head and began thrusting hard in and out of her mouth. At first Karen gagged when his cock touched the back of her throat. Tears dotted the corners of her eyes. To keep from choking, she breathed through her nose and relaxed her throat.

Then he slowed down and pulled completely out of her

———————————————

whereas I could experience with all five senses, an actual physical union with Mandy.

Nevertheless, I recognized a very real threat, for there remained some small doubt about who was really in control. You see, I understood immediately that Alain wasn't content merely to fuck my wife. I saw that his purpose went much deeper. Indeed, he intended to dominate, control and ultimately possess her. He had called her his slut, his beautiful cocksucker, and when he made her beg him to fuck her, she had responded. Clearly she was excited by his demands. The brute force and uncompromising command of his desire provided her with an excuse to pursue her own pleasure and

mouth. "Tell me how much you love sucking my cock," he said. She looked up at him and he slapped her cheek with his penis. "Tell me!"

"I love sucking your big cock," she said, her voice barely a whisper.

"Good girl," he told her, pushing between her lips again and pumping slowly in and out. "Your mouth was made for my cock, but now I want to fuck you." He turned off the shower and grabbed her under the arms, lifting her to a standing position. "Let's get dried off." He stepped out of the shower and handed her a towel. She stared at his erection as he dried himself.

"I wonder if it will fit."

"Don't worry, sweet Karen. I won't hurt you, I promise. We'll go very slowly. I want this to last." He took the towel from her, spread it on the floor, and began kissing her. He pinched her nipples with his fingers and bit at her lip. She kissed him back and grabbed his erection. Then he lowered his head to her breast and licked and sucked

---

fantasy without guilt or inhibition. It wasn't that she *wanted* to spread herself open and beg to be fucked (for she's a good girl and would never do such things on her own), it was that she *must*. And once she had allowed herself to go there, or rather to be taken there, she would find that there was no way back.

In reality, Mandy's new interest was actually an old concern revisited in more graphic and less ambiguous terms. Though it had been many years since my wife and I had discussed the interior workings of our intimate life together, I recalled a time six or seven years earlier, during a vacation in Hawaii when I had continually misread her, leaving us both needlessly frustrated. When we finally

her nipples. "Do you want me to bite them?" he asked, sliding his hand between her legs and fingering her.

"Yes, bite my nipples," she said, surprised at herself. He pushed a finger into her and chewed on her nipples. Her hips shook as he slipped a second finger inside her. "Oh, please, bite them harder," she pleaded.

Suddenly he lowered her to the floor, pushed her legs apart, and kneeled between them. "Spread your pussy open with your hands and ask me to fuck you," he commanded.

Karen shivered with desire and shame as she reached both hands between her legs and opened herself. She'd never done anything like this before, and it excited her so much she began to tremble. The way Alain dominated her made her feel wanton, humiliated, and incredibly alive. More than anything in the world she wanted to be fucked by this man. She rubbed her clitoris and dipped a finger inside her vagina, all the while looking directly into his eyes. "Please fuck me now, Alain," she said, her voice low and husky.

———————————

got around to discussing our lack of communication, I had suggested that in the future it might help matters if she took a more active role in initiating sex, instead of always relying on me to do so. I was surprised at how much she resented and resisted this idea.

"Sex is about power—and someone in a relationship has to assume the dominant role," she'd argued. "Whether you like it or not, I'm submissive and I always have been. You know, as silly as this seems, I'd never even given a blow job before I met you. You showed me almost everything I know about sex, both what you like and what I ought to try, and now, after years of developing our trust and love, you're telling me you no longer want to be in that position.

Alain smiled and guided the head of his penis to her opening. "You're so sexy, Karen, such a sexy slut." He lunged forward, slowly pushing his way into her. Karen cried out, then put her hands on his ass and pulled him deeper. "You're so tight," he said.

"It's been a long time. Just keep going, slowly." He stroked in and out shallowly several times and then pushed again until he was buried inside her as far as he could go. Karen wanted to call out, to scream his name, to bang her head against the wall, to lose consciousness. She felt as if she'd made an unexpected and illegal border crossing and was riding a horse in the wild steppes of Mongolia, drifting down the Amazon in a dugout canoe, heading somewhere unknown.

Alain raised his torso up and stared down at her as he slid his penis rhythmically in and out. Karen moved her hips in circles, rising to meet him. Her breath came in gasps and she moaned in time with their thrusts. That which would have seemed ridiculous, ob-

––––––––

What you don't understand is that for me it's as though years ago you started to open me up and then, at some point, you simply stopped. It was as though you suddenly got frightened and ran away, leaving so much unexplored."

I remember her speech felt like a hard slap across the face. What she'd said was basically true, though I wouldn't admit or accept it. I'd always preferred to think of myself as the adventurous and open-minded one, though in reality, I'd long ago run up against my own set of inhibitions. Past what I assumed were safe and socially acceptable modes of sexual behavior, I was afraid to inflict my fantasies on my partner, for fear my desires would be exposed, re-

scene, even silly to her two days ago, now ruled her. She wanted to scream, "Fuck me, Alain, fuck me with your big cock." There was no playfulness whatsoever in this act, no humor. She was fucking as if her life depended on it.

Alain pulled out and rubbed the head of his penis against her clit, then slipped back inside. "Oh, fuck," she groaned, out loud this time, humping back, "Make me come, Alain." As her orgasm rolled over her, Karen felt Alain tense up and shoot his semen inside her. She hooked her ankles around his waist and pulled him deeper inside with her heels.

"Oh, my God," she kept repeating to herself. This was serious. There was no turning back now. She had really done it.

*   *   *

The next day Alain called to invite her to come to his studio. "I'll be done with my last appointment about three o'clock. You can come then and I'll take some new passport pictures for you. Take a taxi."

———————————————

jected, or even accepted. So I'd learned to be careful what I wished for, keeping my wilder sexual imaginings locked away in the asylum of my psyche. As I grew older and more respectable in my various roles—as husband, father, and professor—the unknown was a threshold I increasingly hesitated to cross. "Why does it always have to be my responsibility?" I replied. "Can't you take a few risks as well?"

"No," she said. "I married you because you were my mentor, my soulmate, my lover. Your strength and decisiveness are what I found most attractive about you. I've always thought a man should know what he wants and pursue it. You should desire me enough to

He gave her the address. "I'll see you then. And Karen, wear something sexy. Those embassy people can be pretty hard to please." She laughed and hung up the phone.

After a long drive through winding streets that climbed the bluffs above the ocean, the taxi driver dropped her off in front of a gate that led into the courtyard of an old building. "It should be through that door," he told her, pointing with his chin. "You may need to ring the bell." Karen thanked him and gave him a generous tip. "Thank you, Madame. Be careful."

She tried the door and found it unlocked, so she pushed through and stepped into the courtyard, where she saw several numbered but otherwise unmarked doors, along with some dirty windows with large shutters. Alain's studio was identified only by his name on a small placard attached to the door. She knocked lightly, but there was no answer, so she turned the knob, opened the door halfway, and leaned into a tiny room cluttered with chairs and a coffee table piled high with magazines. "Alain?" she called out. As

---

tell me exactly what would give you pleasure. Maybe feminists and others would resent that attitude and find it hopelessly passive, a socially conditioned response in this time of strong and independent women, but I don't see it that way. It's simply what I respond to sexually. I'm a violin in search of someone with a bow. I get turned on by being the object of your gratification."

But even though she'd handed me the key, spelled out clearly what she truly desired, I'd done my best to ignore her wishes and go on with our life as before. And now it had finally caught up with me.

Though I could sense where the plot of "The Widow" might be going, I forced myself to keep reading. Though drawn broadly and

her eyes adjusted to the dim light, she saw before her a doorway blocked off by a heavy curtain.

Just then the curtain moved and Alain appeared, dressed in a dark blue apron and wearing rubber gloves. "Karen, come in," he said, smiling. "I was in the darkroom, developing some film. I thought I heard something." He led her through the curtain and into a larger room filled with camera equipment, tripods, lights, screens, a long, low couch, two large armoires, a huge steamer chest, and a shelf filled with hats, shoes, and all kinds of strange props. They passed into a narrow hallway lit with a purple bulb, rounded a corner, pushed through yet another heavy black curtain, and entered the darkroom.

"This is where I develop my film and make prints," he said, touching her arm. "I'm sorry about these gloves. I just need to put these chemicals away, if you don't mind." He guided her toward a row of sinks. In one were negatives of what might be a family portrait. "Why don't you go back into the studio and sit down. I'm

---

without much concrete detail, there was still something vaguely ominous about the setting of Alain's studio. The dusty glass and shutters of the old building seemed to conceal a sinister psychic interior. The space behind the curtain of the studio was like a photographic negative of the colorful and sunlit coastline and city outside. Like the artistic, black-and-white photographs Alain kept catalogued in bound volumes, his studio was a darkroom of ritualized and fetishistic eroticism, of rubber gloves and lace corsets, of complex role-playing and darkly sexual games.

Alain suggested she "make herself at home" in this environment. While she waited for him to finish with his chemicals, she looked at

sorry to keep you waiting. I didn't realize the time. If you want, you can make yourself a cup of tea. There's an electric pot for hot water, some mugs and tea bags on top of the desk in the corner. Make yourself at home. I'll only be a minute."

"Thank you, Alain. I hate to bother you while you work."

"No bother at all. I'll be right with you."

Back in the large room Karen located the desk and plugged in the pot. She sat down at the desk chair and dropped a tea bag into a discolored white ceramic mug. As she waited for the water to boil, she glanced around, noting the desk calendar with the previous month still showing. Finding a tall bookcase nearby, she pulled two large photo albums down and set them on the desk before her. The first contained artistic black-and-white shots of deserted city streets. In one a wind-tossed newspaper was suspended in midair, between the tall facades of buildings, like some ghostly apparition. She flipped through the pages, her eyes delighting in the images. Toward the end of the first book was a series of pictures of bent and

---

his photographs of twisted trees and streets devoid of people. Then Alain appeared and told her he also liked taking pictures of naked women in candid and erotic poses. Showing her his many trunks full of lingerie, costumes, antiques, and props, he suggested that artifice was, for him, the driving force behind all beauty and eroticism.

Then he ordered her to get undressed and masturbate in front of the camera as he took pictures. For a second she hesitated, but his voice commanded her and she began unbuttoning her blouse. Next he moved her through a series of increasingly vulgar and degrading poses, and abused her verbally as she complied. Masturbating next

contorted trees and another of grapevines that resembled the twisted knuckles of an old man's hand.

The second book contained images of objects arranged in still-life settings. There were many pictures of bottles and glasses, some half full, others empty. One shot portrayed a tipped-over wineglass surrounded by a reflecting pool of dark liquid. As she flipped the pages, other objects appeared, including a charged series based on black-and-white shots of women's lingerie. In one the photographer had focused upon a corset, the garters of which were hooked to empty stockings that hung over the edge of the table.

Karen was so engaged in her contemplation of this image that she didn't notice when Alain appeared behind her. She jumped at the sound of his voice. "I see you've found my work," he said.

"You startled me." She laughed nervously. Alain leaned forward and looked over her shoulder.

"You know I've taken that same picture many times with many

---

to her, he ejaculated on her face just as she reached her own orgasm.

That night at dinner Alain told her that, after she had given her permission, he would be taking full possession of her. Without hesitation she agreed to his proposal, and he immediately changed her name to "Gigi" and gave her a dog collar to wear around her neck to symbolize her subservient condition. When he drove her back to her hotel, he made her unbutton her dress and remove her bra in the car. He told her to go upstairs to her room and pack, and to wait for him in the lobby the next morning, when he would come for her. He instructed her to expose her breasts to the night clerk when

different models, but none has ever matched the intensity of the fleshless one. What do you think of it?"

"It's very powerful, very compelling somehow. I'm not quite sure why—the angle, I suppose, and the way the light through the lace plays against those shadows. You've made it seem alive. It's shocking and at the same time very beautiful. I . . . I don't know what else to say."

"Would you like to see it?"

"I . . ." Karen could hear the water boiling in the pot on the desk next to her. "I'm not sure . . ."

"The corset. I've got it here. In the trunk by the armoire. I'll get it for you." He walked to the trunk and opened it. "I've got all kinds of dresses and clothing, lots of antiques and props. I take pictures of women, too, if you haven't already seen." He waved at the photo albums.

"No, this one's full of trees and city streets."

"Well, many of the others contain nude studies, some very can-

---

she walked past him on the way to the stairs. She did exactly as he had ordered.

Afterward, locked in her room, she realized that, by allowing her to return to her room for the night, he had given her one last chance to change her mind. Though her passport was still missing, she contemplated leaving the hotel and taking a train to Paris, then flying home.

The text ended with her wondering what to do. Though a part of me hoped that Karen would have the good sense to leave while she could, in reality I knew that things had already gone too far and there was no going back.

did and erotic. To me, there's nothing more beautiful than the fe-male form. Ah, here it is." He carried the black lace corset back to Karen and handed it to her. "Put it on," he said.

"I don't know. . . ."

"Do it, Karen. Right now." His voice was firm. "Come over by the couch in front of the screen and take your clothes off." He took her by the hand and guided her into position. "Unbutton your blouse," he said, adjusting a light behind her. Then he moved to a camera mounted on a tripod.

Karen stared at the camera as she opened the front of her blouse. She heard the lens click as she dropped the blouse on the floor. "Good, Karen, now unhook your bra." She did as he told her, dis-playing her breasts for the camera. "Lean forward and cup them in your hands. Yes, that's good. Perfect. Now take off your jeans."

When she stood naked before him, Alain told her to bend over the couch and show her ass. "Spread the cheeks with your hands so the camera can see your pussy and your asshole. You are a slut for

---

I was pretty sure that the next day she'd be waiting for him when Alain came to her hotel. I imagined he'd take her to his studio, where he'd hand her a pile of clothes and focus his video camera on her. "I want you to get undressed and change into these clothes. I'm taking you to Toulon this evening to get a tattoo," he'd tell her. Once she was naked, he'd order her to follow him into the bathroom. "You'll need to shave all the hair off your pussy. And I'm going to make a little video of you for my friend Hubert, who's got a collection of tapes with women shaving. Don't ask me why. I guess it turns him on. Just make sure you get it nice and smooth and don't cut yourself."

By now I was typing furiously at the keyboard.

this camera, no?" he asked. As she posed, Karen became increasingly excited. She hardly knew what she was doing anymore, hardly recognized herself in her behavior. She knew only that exposing herself so completely and following his commands turned her on. She pulled on her nipples as he took picture after picture. Then he told her to lie on her back on the couch with her legs spread. "Show me how you play with yourself when I'm not around."

Karen shuddered as she pressed her fingers against her wetness. She found her clit and shook violently, climaxing after only a few seconds. "Very nice, Karen. I got your passport photos as you were having an orgasm. Now let me get you something more fun to play with." He went to the trunk and pulled out a large, realistic-looking rubber cock. "Let's see you fuck yourself with this."

Karen took the dildo from him and rubbed it against her wet crotch. She pressed the soles of her feet together and watched herself push the thick head of the artificial penis past her slick opening. "Oh, my," she gasped, and began pumping the object slowly in

---

In Toulon, Alain would take her to an American-style bar he knew of down by the port, where they'd drink whiskey sours until she told him she felt light-headed. "You're going to need the alcohol to help numb the pain," he'd say. "Have one more and then we'll go." He'd made her wear a short jean skirt, a tight T-shirt with a plunging neckline, and open-toed sandals with high heels. More than one French sailor had already noticed that she wasn't wearing a bra or panties.

The tattoo shop would be a squalid little hole that catered to drunken sailors on shore leave. Alain would order her to sit in the chair with her legs spread and her skirt hiked up around her waist

and out. She closed her eyes and pleasured herself, floating from one plateau to the next. "I'm going to come again," she announced, rubbing her clitoris with her free hand. Just then she felt something warm and soft against her cheek. She opened her eyes and saw Alain standing over her, his cock in his hand.

"Keep going," he told her. She shuddered with the beginning of her own orgasm as the first hot splash of semen rained over her cheek, splashing onto her forehead and hair. She rolled her hips as he milked his sperm over her lips and chin. "My slut," he pronounced as he rubbed his cock over her wet face.

When they were done, Alain told her to put the corset and stockings on. "Now it's time to take your picture lying back on the table."

*   *   *

That night, over dinner at a quiet restaurant, Alain told Karen he needed to talk seriously with her. "*Cherie,* you and I know this affair between us can only go to one place," he said, holding her hand

---

while his "old friend" Marcel prepared his inks and needles. As drunk as she was, she'd still burn with shame when a group of sailors in French navy uniforms and little caps with red pom-poms crowded into the shop to watch.

When Marcel was ready, he'd rub alcohol over the sensitive skin she'd shaved earlier, then carefully write the letters S-L-U-T in neat and tiny capital letters on her pubis. Of course Alain would be thoughtful enough to translate for the sailors, who'd roar out their approval. The pricking of the needles would be far worse than she'd imagined it might be, though it wouldn't take long to ink the four

across the table. "But I can tell you're not confident or even sure exactly where that place is." He smiled, and took a sip of wine. "So I'm going to tell you, but first you must promise me that you will not interrupt or speak a word until I am finished." Karen looked at him and nodded her head.

"Good. Understand, then, dear Karen, that with your full understanding, permission, and consent, I am going to take complete possession of you. From now on I will tell you where to live, what to eat, how or even if you may dress. In fact, I'm going to change your name, right now, from this moment on, to Gigi. So you see, Gigi, that I will control and rule over every aspect of your life. You will give your body to me to do as I wish with it." His eyes never left hers. When he reached across the table and pinched one of her nipples hard through her dress, it was like being shocked with an electric prod.

"Understand that this is simply our little game. Like life itself, it's far too intense and dangerous to last long, so it must be enjoyed in

---

small letters. By then the sailors would have pressed in close for a better view. Despite her discomfort, everyone would be having a wonderful time.

I found that I was really getting into the spirit of Mandy's fiction, and so I unzipped my fly and pressed on with the narrative, giving free reign to my imagination.

The following day Alain would take her to live at the villa of a rich friend of his. He'd blindfold her in the car on the way so she wouldn't know exactly where she was going. In the coming days and weeks Karen would come to understand that Alain and his

the present. Keep in mind that you can always refuse. If I tell you to do something that is beyond the scope of your desire, then all you must do is say no. I won't ask twice nor listen to any explanations or excuses. If you refuse me, the game will be over, the spell broken, and we will immediately go our separate ways. Now, Gigi, what do you say?"

"Yes."

"Fine, then." He took a small box from the pocket of his jacket and handed it to her. "Open this." Inside was a black leather dog collar embellished with silver studs. "Put it on now and don't ever take it off." Though her heart was pounding in her chest and she could barely swallow once the collar was in place, she did as she was told.

In the car on the way back from the restaurant, Alain informed her that he would come to her hotel in the morning to pick her up. She would have her bags packed and be in the lobby waiting. "But for now I want you to unbutton your dress and take off your bra.

---

friends were deeply involved in the world of pornography, prostitution, and organized crime.

One night they'd throw a party for some business associates. Alain would insist she help with the entertainment. Stripped naked, blindfolded, tattooed, her hands tied to the metal headboard of a huge bed, the men would take turns with her while Alain watched and videotaped everything. Most of the guests would finish on her face, her breasts, or her belly. When it was over, Alain would unlock the handcuffs and take the blindfold off. He'd bring her a washcloth, a bowl of warm water, some soap, and a towel. "Did you enjoy yourself?" he'd ask.

Give it to me," he said, when she'd finished. She handed him the bra and he tossed it over his shoulder into the backseat. "Leave the dress unbuttoned."

Several minutes later he pulled the car in front of the hotel and told her to walk through the lobby and up the stairs to her room with her breasts partially exposed. "Make sure you open the front of your dress all the way when you go past the night clerk there behind the desk," he told her. "He's a young guy with a round face who often hangs around at the Café Henri, where I sometimes stop in for a drink. Everybody there calls him Bébé. So be a good slut now, Gigi, and go show Bébé your nice big titties. And make sure he gets a good look, because I'm going to call him later and ask him all about it." He squeezed her nipple again as she opened the car door.

Her pulse racing and cold sweat dripping from her armpits, Karen pushed her way purposefully through the heavy front doors of the hotel and strode across the lobby toward the front desk and the stairs beyond. She could feel the bored clerk's eyes light up and

---

"Yes."

Suddenly I couldn't take any more. I could see clearly where things were going. It was bad enough to have let another man take possession of my wife. I couldn't just stand by helplessly while he turned her into a whore. I realized that the two of them had left me no choice but to resort to violence. Once I came to the decision, Alain was as good as dead.

The next day I left my campus office early enough that I'd arrive home just a few minutes after Mandy. When I got there I could tell she was already in the den, as her car was parked in the driveway and I could see the light on through the blinds. I

focus on her as she moved closer. *"Bonsoir, monsieur,"* she said, pulling her dress open so that her breasts were completely exposed to his view. As she moved past the desk and toward the stairwell, she looked quickly back over her shoulder toward the street, but the dark car was already gone.

Inside her room she pushed a chair up against the locked door. What was she doing? All of this was insanity. She sat on the edge of the bed and hugged herself. She wanted to laugh out loud and cry at the same time. Her hands were shaking as she slowly buttoned her dress, then reached up to her neck and touched the leather collar. Her thoughts spun wildly in her head. Her daughter had married a dentist in California. Her husband was dead and buried. Her passport and her driver's license had been stolen. This evening she'd willingly consented to become the possession of a complete stranger in a foreign country. Who was she? She really didn't know, anymore. Nevertheless, she could feel the blood pulsing through her veins, screaming that she was alive.

---

left my car down the street a ways and quietly let myself into the house.

Sure enough I could hear Mandy's fingers clicking on the keyboard. I closed the front door behind me and started silently down the hall, my right hand in my bulging coat pocket. I'd had enough of her double life, her lies and fictions. I was going to catch her in the act and put an end to it once and for all.

She didn't notice me slip into the room or sneak up behind her. Once I got hold of her, she never had a chance. I pulled the handcuffs from my pocket, slapped one over her wrist, and, twisting her arm behind her back, pulled her roughly out of the chair and into a

When she finally calmed down, she realized that, by allowing her to return to the hotel, Alain had given her a last chance to change her mind. Even without her papers, she had enough money to catch a train to Paris and straighten the mess out at the U.S. embassy there. In a matter of a few short days she could be back among familiar faces. All she had to do was settle her account with the clerk downstairs to whom she'd just exposed herself, walk out the hotel door, and keep moving. No one would ever be the wiser.

---

standing position. Then I bent her forward over the desk, and locked her other wrist into the handcuffs. With my foot, I pushed the chair across the room on its casters and grabbed my wife roughly by the hair. I made her stare at the flickering monitor as I chose "select all" from the edit menu of the word processor. Then I hit the delete key and quickly chose "save."

It was over in an instant.

I pressed Mandy down to her knees, and unzipped my fly.

Lips trembling, she looked at me with wide eyes.

"You belong to me," I said.

shadow
of a
man

William Harrison

1

In the year before Mandela was released from prison and the last months before white rule ended, Cal Vega went to South Africa to photograph a client in Johannesburg. His clients were still paying inflated prices for his portraits in those days, so he traveled in style, staying at the best hotels and living, as he was fond of saying, single and superficial.

That morning it was the Carlton, and he stood at the window of his suite gazing out at the skyscrapers of the city. His own face was mirrored there, too: a lean craggy face over forty years of age, no longer young, yet dark and handsome enough—with something of the predator about it—so that women knew what he wanted and often gave it to him. He watched the street below his window—Wanderer's Street, a great name—and gave it his professional appraisal as if he meant to snap it with a wide-angle lens, then he looked at himself again and the furniture of the room behind him: a layered effect, things superimposed, reflections on reflections. The city was like Dallas, where he grew up: generally clean, busy, and windblown. He felt energetic and confident in the way Americans, perhaps Texans in particular, often feel in foreign countries.

And certain that a new woman would show up.

One always did.

His client lived in Saxonwald, a suburb of bright garden estates beneath a canopy of eucalyptus and cottonwood trees. The villa was near the zoo, so occasionally a lion's muffled roar drifted in with the sounds of distant traffic and the clacking precision of all the lawn sprinklers.

Cal made his appearance in a yellow leather jacket and jeans, carrying his camera bags and presenting his business card. The card read, simply, Calvin Vega, and that said it all: portrait photographer, famous enough, expensive.

A little gray servant took the camera bags, set them inside the front door, and hurried away with the card. Eventually Cal was ushered through a portico and into a garden where General Hofmyr awaited him.

"Hello, my young friend," the general said, sweeping out his arm. "Can we do our work out here? This is my parade field these days. You like roses? How about an outdoor photograph?"

"My specialty is the close-up," Cal answered. "But we can talk about it."

They shook hands as the general said, "Flowers and gardening clothes, that's my thought. So how long will this take?"

"If you're busy, I can come back."

"Oh no, very unbusy. Retired. My daughter arranged all this, you know. Says you want a dear price for it."

"I have two prices," Cal said, using an old line. "For work in focus and work out of focus. The pictures out of focus are called art, so they naturally cost more."

The general understood and laughed, placing his pruning shears on a stone wall.

"We're having lunch soon. My daughter instructed me to commandeer you for lunch. Hope it suits you."

"Sure, we'll use the afternoon light."

"And maybe you want to psychoanalyze me before you take my photo? To get the hidden self. Is that what you do?"

"No, none of that. We just pose you. And we discuss it, but in the end we do it my way."

"It's my face, but we do it your way?"

"You're only the subject."

"Like Picasso and his mistress, is it?"

"Exactly like that," Cal replied evenly.

His clients were wealthy, but their wealth varied. General Hofmyr was clearly one of the lesser clients, and the fee for a portrait was perhaps something of a sacrifice. The villa was moderate in size, perhaps fifteen rooms with servants' quarters, pool house, and garden, but not without the need of paint and minor repairs. Oleander and roses camouflaged chipped masonry and missing tiles. The sitting rooms beyond the garden had a seedy look, and their brass and silver lacked a military luster, so speculation became the game. Who wanted this portrait at fancy prices? Some organization? No, probably not, because few organizations would want to impress anybody with the Vega signature. Maybe the daughter? And, if so, why?

Before lunch they sat in a musty study overflowing with crowded bookshelves and stacks of dust-covered magazines. Occupying the space above the hearth was a nineteenth-century oil painting of the battle of Blood River: Zulu warriors with their spears, Voortrekkers, cattle, wagons in a circle, brass cannon, an officer brandishing a pistol, and all the dead lying around a hippo pool in an eddy of the river. The painter had no particular talent, but the action had zest, a kind of B-movie breathlessness.

"Want your portrait with medals and braid and all that?"

"I've outgrown my uniforms," the old man grunted. "Besides, I fought with the British army in the real war. I've had nothing to do with these skirmishes in recent years—Angola and Caprivi and all that. Hell, I'm old. I knew Jan Smuts. I was a South African when we chose between Hitler and the Allies. There were supporters, you know, on both sides down here—at least until the madman marched into the Netherlands."

The general had a stubble of ashen beard, so needed a shave before sitting for his portrait. He was oddly soft, and Cal had expected a baron with a swagger stick, something more severe, not this.

"I really don't know about politics," Cal admitted.

"Such a luxury, not to fret over politics!"

"Yes, but I suppose we should talk about posing for pictures instead."

"By all means. My daughter says to talk aesthetics—the ideas of photography, all that. She knows your reputation with women, I believe, from the magazines."

"The exaggerations of magazine writers have been good for my business," Cal allowed, shrugging.

"My daughter married a businessman who never liked me. They're divorced now, alimony and all that, and I think she wants my career on show for reasons of her own. As for me, well, I have a curious premonition about this portrait."

"A premonition?"

"Hm, a creepy feeling that it will somehow show me for what I am. Sounds crazy, I know."

"I hear this all the time," Cal assured him. "A lot of people fear that others will see secrets in their faces."

"Like kaffirs in the bush: don't want their photos snapped and their souls robbed. Yes, we've all heard that. Don't put any stock in it, do you?"

"Afraid not," Cal replied, smiling.

"Mind you, I'm not superstitious. I was an intuitive officer, but never superstitious. Yet I'm uneasy with this picture taking."

"You don't have to do it. You can tell your daughter that you didn't like me and won't have any of it."

"Oh, no, we'll go through with it. So my daughter can have her lunch with you. I think she wants to rub an ankle against your leg underneath the table. Just to check out your reputation."

"Is it time for lunch?"

"It is. Come on."

They walked through the portico into a room of high windows, skylights, and a table brightened with bowls of salad and shiny wineglasses with good silver.

"It isn't a premonition exactly," said the general, returning to the subject. "Tell me this, though: Do you ever see in your photographs something that didn't seem to be there as you took the picture?"

Cal picked up an olive from a dish, ate it, then turned the wet seed in his fingers.

"I don't think about that sort of thing," he answered.

"But you're a professional. And, hm, take so many photos. You must've thought about it."

Cal smirked. "There have been a number of, oh, philosophers of photography," he said. "They usually ponder the obvious. Intellectuals. All intellectuals are usually, you know, intensely stupid. I mean, a photograph by its nature is superficial. And most of the so-called artists with the camera use the same technique: They take thousands of exposures, thousands, and only rarely will a picture have anything special about it. This afternoon I'll get you from dozens of angles, and we'll hope one of them flatters you. That's all my work is."

"You don't much believe in your own craft."

"Belief has no part of it. I like photography without all the intellectual shit. And women who don't talk too much. And travel without, oh, you know, too many destinations."

"Well argued, not that I believe you," the general told him.

"The camera lens is inferior to the human eye," Cal went on. "It doesn't actually see much. It distorts. It's too mechanical. Don't give it much credit."

He tossed the olive pit on the table: a casual gesture that somehow underscored his indifference. It landed beside a silver dish.

They turned to the sound of high heels on the patio.

"Ellen," said the general, greeting his daughter. She was a slender woman in her late thirties, blonde with a page boy cut, wearing a silk dress and carrying an Italian handbag. Cal saw that she was probably one of those rare women who looked better naked than clothed, and she moved like liquid as if she knew this herself.

"You made a good choice," said the general during introductions. "I like your American photographer—although he doesn't believe in discussing the magic in his craft."

When she smiled at Cal for the first time, he knew what was plainly there: She wanted a piece of him.

At lunch she asked direct questions.

"Have you ever been married?"

"Oh no, always a bachelor," he told her, and she covered that question with a flurry of conversation with her father.

He later caught her examining his face and hair, so she asked, "Do you go to women hairstylists or men?"

He waited a beat, then answered, "Women. And I like them to lean against me while they work."

She smiled and wanted more white wine, so the general summoned the little gray houseman who went searching for some. Her eyes flashed with mischief, as if she might be far ahead of what she actually said or did. Intelligent, Cal knew. Her eyes told on her.

"You published a book of nude studies," Ellen began once more. "Do you still photograph nudes?"

"Sure," he came back. "Wanta pose for me?"

The old man paid elaborate attention to his chicken salad.

"Possibly," she answered. "What do you have in mind? Something discreet or something for the girlie magazines?"

"You decide," Cal said, grinning, and the general snorted with laughter.

"I'd like something scandalous," said Ellen, her fork poised beside her face. "But pornography isn't really scandalous these days, is it?"

"No," Cal admitted. "But, damn, we could try."

She laughed out loud with her head thrown back. The curve of her neck, he decided, was hot enough by itself.

———

At the afternoon portrait session the old man wanted even more conversation, so had to be asked several times to sit quietly.

"Turn just so," Cal instructed him. "We want, you know, a Vermeer effect: the light put on without its source."

"See, you take technique very seriously," General Hofmyr noted.

"That's beside the point," Cal assured him. "This is just scrub work—like flying airplanes or driving buses. If it has any glamour or importance to anyone, it's because I'm getting overpaid. Like that: The pilot makes more money than the bus driver, so he's more glamorous. There, keep your chin at that angle."

The general had been persuaded to wear a dark suit and tie, to sit indoors, and to allow his craggy face to become the featured object. He sat beside a window in good light. A mahogany chair and a pale tapestry were his props except for the book in his hand, a thin military memoir written long ago, his only written work, and it would remain or disappear as Cal decided how to crop the finished portrait.

"Do I look like a warrior?"

"Keep still," Cal replied, and he wanted to say, no, you look like somebody's gentle grandfather.

"You're very pragmatic and cynical, aren't you?" the general asked him. "But there's a school of thought that photography can be great—the same as paintings by the old masters."

"Sit quietly, please," Cal told him, smiling, and the old Hasselblad made its little noise.

2

They stood on Platform 16 waiting to board the Blue Train.

She had business at the Cape, she said, and asked him to come with her. It was a sexual dare, clearly, so he naturally said yes.

Like all the other women on the luxury train, Ellen dressed in high heels, the Fendi scarf, the whole ta da, while Cal wore his jeans and leather jacket. She wouldn't look at him while they waited—as if she might break out in laughter if she did. He decided she was definitely hot, but loaded with karma: secrets and troubles he would never ask about.

Their compartment had fresh flowers and a chilled bottle of Cape wine. While he stuffed his photographic gear and bags into the top of the closet, she took off her shoes.

The train pulled out of the station's shadows into a bright and windy day. On the outskirts of the city he saw several yellowish mounds—each the size of a football stadium—and smelled the odor.

"Cyanide," she told him. "Residue from the old gold mines. They used tons of it to leach the gold away from the rock, and now the wind carries the dust, everyone getting his nose and eyes burned, and everybody sort of, um, waiting around in the poison nowadays for things to get worse."

The skyscrapers became glints on the horizon, and the veldt opened up: scrubby prairie like West Texas with low bushes and red clay fields littered with stones. A windmill passed, the only object in the flat landscape.

A short time later they sat in the dining car for lunch, awaiting the afternoon pleasures. He remembered a magazine assignment in South Africa years ago—his only other visit—when he went up to Kruger Park with a guide provided by the tourist board. Although he went to photograph the animals, the guide, Jill, posed for him openly and wantonly, giving herself to him in the VW van, in lodges, in tents, and on the lime grass beneath a thorn tree where a wandering lion might have strolled by to gobble them up in their distracted frenzy. Jill, yes: He wrote her name on the backs of the photos he made of her and some of them fell out of a book years later.

"What're you thinking about?" Ellen asked.

"My first visit here years ago. Kruger Park."

"I was wondering about the size of your cock."

"Adequate," he told her. "About the size of two beer cans."

She laughed and rolled a spoon around in her soup.

A soft underworld of women. He sometimes hired traveling companions, girls from the escort services, but usually he didn't have to. More often they appeared like this. Maybe something in his appraising glance turned them on, but who could say? Sexual communication was never a subtle business: a glance, a physical presence, recognitions learned by teenagers and occasionally perfected by a few devotees of the sport.

In his university days he fell in with the arty crowd. His photos were always girls, and his pretentious friends called them nudes, wanting to see what he had in his darkroom, and he moved around the campus like a celebrity. Some of the early pictures appeared in his first published volume. The Vega signature. And his name became known, and he was also Cal, Calvin, Cocky, darling, shugah, and names that came from strangers and less than strangers. The girls and their poses: girls whose gazes were pensive as poets and others, wide open and brazen, who might have resulted in his arrest.

In the dining car of the Blue Train he sat with Ellen, watching her watch him. She had a veneer of elegance about her, and he recalled an Austin socialite who came on to him. She wanted a Rachmaninoff fuck, but he gave her "Night Train" instead, bracing her up against the wall of his darkroom while he took her from behind.

For a while he had money, mobility, and a career filled with assignments, but he was flippant about photography as art and described his work to a television interviewer as Lyric Titties. His pals laughed, but later a critic used it against him, and if he conspired to condemn himself as a serious photographer, he was satisfied when his work spiraled down into portrait work. He lived in New York, part of a group of young cockbirds and their girlfriends, who gave their inebriated grins to Lincoln Center and the bistros. Portraits of the rich became his constant, the arty stuff all gone, and women became the currency he made and spent. He moved back to Texas, then to Malibu, then back to Texas again, and life was a series of projects, temporary alignments, and copulation or one of the several good substitutes. There was nothing pathological to it, he claimed, not at all; it was comedy, it was bachelorhood.

After coffee and a mint he and Ellen made their way back to their compartment. He set up a tripod because she wanted to play artist and model, and he suspected she might play movie director in bed: go here, more of that, scenarios for every occasion.

"What's your business at the Cape?" he asked as she removed her shoes.

"A party. Maybe more than one. And I want to, um, show you off. My social prize, do you mind? Also, I have a beach house at Clifton, so we can swim."

"Good, I'll photograph the ocean."

"The ocean needs attention," she agreed, smiling. "I'll undress now if that's all right."

"Absolutely."

As she unbuttoned herself he slowly unbuckled his belt, pushed off his shoes, and slipped out of his jeans and briefs. Her eyes fixed on his nakedness.

And yes: She was far more beautiful without clothes. The rib cage and narrow waist. Large breasts with raised nipples. She stood and stretched, pulling her breasts high, then stepped out of her panties. Her mound wore a soft, light, delicate hair and not much of it: the cunt of a child, small and pouting.

He neglected the camera and moved toward her, taking off his shirt. She propped her legs apart on the couch.

"Here's my ocean," she said in a hoarse whisper. "And I see you like it."

3

He had seen Cape Town once before, those years ago, but it was better than he remembered it: the great monolith of Table Mountain hovering over it, the crystal bay, flowers everywhere. A city perched on the edge of civilization: a space station brightly adorned on the dark continent. He had an impulse to take photos of it, but knew that would reduce its impact.

They took a taxi around Sea Point, then went on toward Clifton and a stretch of highway where, on their right, the villas clung to the cliffs below them. At one of these cliffside houses they turned through an arch and drove directly onto the rooftop parking space. As he paid the driver and gathered luggage, he heard seabirds wheeling and screeching overhead and could smell the soft rot of the salt breeze. The rooftop railings were sculpted with oleander and jacaranda. Beside their blossoms sat an old Jeep partially covered with tarpulin.

"While I run my errands the next couple of days, that's your vehicle," Ellen said, pointing to it.

They made their way down a metal staircase into a house of

white boxes and rectangles fitted into the rocky cliffside. The main room featured a wall of glass facing the ocean: a view miles out into the Atlantic. Books and magazines strewn around. Indian rugs and leather couches. A Tiffany lamp with a blue scarf draped over it. On a teakwood table beside a jade Buddha there was also a shiny 9 mm pistol and a clip of bullets.

She caught him looking at it.

"There's a leopard in the neighborhood," she explained.

"A leopard? You're kidding."

She strolled into the kitchen, opened the blinds, and set out tumblers for drinks. "A few of the neighbors have actually, um, seen it. They say it's a big beautiful cat. It comes down from the mountain at night to raid the rubbish bins and sometimes kills and eats a neighborhood pet. What're we going to do this afternoon?"

He watched the afternoon sun catch her face in a nimbus of orange, and she returned his smile with her own. When he kissed her, she leaned into him and opened her mouth.

"As long as I'm around you," she told him, whispering in his ear, "I'll never, ever wear panties."

"You're just saying that so I'll do you."

"Play like we're brother and sister," she whispered. "I'm fifteen years old and you're just fourteen. Our parents are drunks and never know anything. Every night I come to your room."

They found their way to a wide leather chair, and she straddled him. When he was awkward getting his jeans open and exposing himself, she teased him. "Come on, little brother. Hurry," she whispered hoarsely.

She went on with the story, riding him, telling him she liked to spy on him in the bathroom while he showered and masturbated.

"This is our favorite chair," she went on, moving with oiled grace. Maybe she'd used the fantasy before, whispering in someone else's ear, but he didn't care. She moved like a belly dancer, thrusting in a steady rhythm, the muscles working below her rib cage, and he felt himself coming, oblivious, bubbling up like lava out of a volcano, and she was whispering all along, telling her story, acting her part, urging him to be a good little brother and a good audience.

The restaurant, later, was called Blue: a candlelit spot on the hillside above the Cape highway. As they finished a bottle of wine after the meal, Cal brought up the subject of the troubles. He mentioned it casually, not really knowing the players: tribal leaders, churchmen, politicians, Brits, or Afrikaaners.

"Um, no, please, not tonight," Ellen responded. "Tonight there's no slum called Crossroads, no secret police, no tribes, just us. But I will tell you about the poet bomber."

"Oh? And who's that?"

"Nobody knows who he is. But he rigs his bombs in high places on crowded streets so that his couplets explode and come raining down. According to his literary critics, he writes fair iambic pentameter. Last week a blast of poetry went off at the top of a flagpole in Longmarket Street. Shattered a few windows."

"And the police can't catch him?"

"No, bloody grand, isn't it? He just composes a few, um, revolutionary verses and mixes in the right amount of explosives. No one ever gets hurt—at least not so far."

"But a guy could get killed around a poetry grenade," Cal offered.

"Ah, but to die for one's art!" she said in mock awe, and they had a laugh.

Back at the cliffside house she strolled into the bedroom, shedding her clothes as she went. "You're the gardener and very, um, dirty. Your fingernails are black and you smell like fertilizer and sweat. You asked to come in the house for a drink, but I want more and I'll pay you a little extra."

She perched herself on the thick pillows at the head of the bed, opened her legs, and began massaging herself. As he undressed she bit her lower lip, closed her eyes with pleasure, and kept doing herself. He walked on his knees across the bed and joined her, letting his fingers rest softly on hers, feeling her rhythms, then he leaned into her, penetrated that wet little vagina, and rode with her as the headboard bumped against the wall. He loved it, playing the gardener and feeling like more of a witness than Cal the participant.

Later they lay in each other's arms, and when he told her how beautiful she was, she answered, no, not really, my mother was very beautiful, and I've only been a bit pretty. He asked her about her parents and if she had a brother. The question made her laugh.

"A brother? Oh, no, that was just a little game we played. I didn't actually have a brother!"

He asked about her father, too.

"He's an old dear," she offered. "But he never liked my friends or my opinions on anything. He was a hero, you know. Lots of medals. Everyone knew him, but that was years ago. World War Two. And the portrait, well, I want it to remind people who he was. And on the selfish side I want to be, um, thought of as the general's daughter. Is that bad of me?"

"Not at all," he assured her.

"Do you shoot fashion models?" she suddenly asked him.

"Hm, sometimes. In the past."

"I think models are so sad. Beautiful and sad."

"They're definitely sad," he agreed.

"Beauty is a curse, you realize," she said, sighing. "My mother spent her life being beautiful. And sometimes I think places are cursed with their beauty, too. As if, um, the beautiful places on earth have a way of turning us into fools and fanatics. Like Bavaria with all its lovely forests and mountains somehow had a part in making the Third Reich happen. You think I'm right in this?"

"Sure, maybe," he replied. "But men also fight over ugly, worthless pieces of ground, too, don't they?"

"They do, yes," she agreed, turning against him so that their breath mingled. "But a beautiful homeland makes feelings run so deep. The territorial thing. A South African farmer can think of his land and get tears in his eyes."

"Are you that way, too?"

"I love my country. And it's dreadfully beautiful and so—well, so deceptive and troublesome."

Ending the reverie, she smiled and kissed his nose. Then she closed her eyes and drifted toward sleep. Propped on an elbow, he lay there watching her, feeling a peaceful rapture with this good-humored, intelligent, and wanton woman. In the morning, he thought, I'll call my answering service in the States, but I won't go back just yet.

4

He slept ten hours that night, and when he awoke, she had left him a note saying that her errands would be finished by noon. The note lay beneath the keys to the old Jeep.

Instead of calling his service or looking for a darkroom for rent—the general's portrait could wait, he decided—he drove the Jeep to an open café near Bantry Bay, where he had breakfast, then drove to Sea Point and strolled around the sea wall. Young white surfers and their girlfriends lolled on the beach drinking beer, their vague eyes straying off toward the breakers. Under a concrete bridge two boys—a surly white and a smirking Indian, both maybe eleven years old—smoked a joint and gave him a hard glance as he passed. An old black couple, arm in arm, prosperous, balanced their ice-cream cones as they sauntered along the row of palm trees.

A newspaper kiosk had a copy of *Texas Monthly*—a small South African surprise—so he bought it along with the newspapers.

It was more than an hour before noon when he drove back to

Ellen's, parked on the roof, and made his way back down the winding stairs into the house. He turned the key in the lock and entered the main room.

A man in a light brown suit stood beside the coffee table.

"Hello," said the stranger, turning. "And who are you?"

"A friend of Ellen's," Cal answered. "Who're you and how'd you get in?"

"Take it easy. I'm Tom Steyn. Here, see, I've got a key, too."

"Ellen's not here," Cal told him.

"Right, she's not. And you're, ah, what? The new boyfriend?"

"Cal Vega," Cal answered, crossing to the coffee table and dropping his magazine and newspapers there. The pistol, he noted, was absent, and a brown envelope occupied the table.

"That's for Ellen," Steyn said, gesturing toward the envelope. "I just came by to drop it off. American, are you? With a Texas accent, I believe."

Cal nodded. The telltale magazine lay between them, so Steyn was observant and quick. He was also a big man, red-faced with a heavy mustache. When he grinned, the broken capillaries in his face became radiant. He spoke with a deep Afrikaaner baritone and resembled a singer in a barbershop quartet, yet there was a certain menace and authority to him.

"How do you like our country?"

"Love it. This is my second visit. I was here years ago."

"Ah, you come here on business?"

"I'm a portrait photographer. I just did Ellen's father in Johannesburg."

"Ah, sure, and how's the general?"

"I'm sure you keep up with him."

"Actually, I've been working almost exclusively with Ellen, but I can't anymore. The packet explains that. Lovely here at the Cape this time of year, don't you agree?"

"Very pretty."

"You should take the drive down to Cape Point. The flowers are all in bloom. You should go, really. We're at our best just now. The troubles in our country, they just fade away at this time of year. Fade away. We have things in hand, you know."

Cal couldn't determine what was wrong. Steyn was perhaps three inches over six feet, maybe 250 pounds, florid and out of shape, yet he wore his khaki suit like a tailored uniform. Was he one of Ellen's lovers? *God,* Cal thought, *she must have dozens.*

"I'd like to visit with Ellen, but I can't stay," Steyn went on. "Tell her I stopped off to leave the packet. Cal Vega, is it? Is that a Mexican name?" He smiled, and those capillaries in his cheeks became a crimson blotch. Betrayed, Cal decided, by a blush. Steyn was uncomfortable, but hiding it as best as he could.

"My father was Mexican and my mother Irish."

"Ah, I see. Now Texas: That's a place I'd like to visit. The Houston Space Center. Cowboys. JR's ranch in Dallas. Or is that just a show on the telly?"

"Just a show," Cal answered, knowing that Steyn knew this very well. At the door they shook hands and said their good-byes.

Afterward Cal strolled back to the coffee table and stared at the envelope. It was sealed, but he wanted to open it.

Finally he sat down with the newspapers and magazine. Who was that guy? He saw in the *Cape Times* that the poet bomber had struck again: a loud and harmless blast in a mall. Glass everywhere, but no injuries. The poetry, translated from the Afrikaans for

English-speaking readers, was filled with lines like "the stem of nightshade erupts into morning," a sort of sophomoric Zen warrior earnestness.

The old issue of *Texas Monthly* brought back a few memories: chicken-fried steak at Threadgill's, a pal named Chigger, Shiner and Lone Star, Rosa's Tex-Mex, and the drawling humor. After a time he put the magazine aside and gazed out on his Atlantic vista. For better or worse, he knew, he was much the same: scoring, dodging, moving on through a landscape of assorted snapshots without theme. He wished Ellen would come back for a long afternoon rut.

She soon pushed through the door with a bag of groceries. Cal took the bag from her arms, kissed her, and followed her into the kitchen.

"You went out, too," she said. "You have today's newspapers."

Her voice was light and airy, and she seemed glad to see him.

"Yeah, and your poet bomber is loose again."

"I heard about it. In the shopping mall."

She put items away in the kitchen as he told her, "There was a guy in the house when I came back. Said he has his own key. Tom Steyn. He left an envelope for you."

"Oh?" she replied casually as she worked.

"Big guy. Said he was a friend."

She turned to him with a smile that somehow failed. "Where's the envelope?" she asked, and it was more important than she wanted him to detect.

"In there on the table," he replied, trying to ignore her secrets. For an instant he felt surprised at himself for wanting to know her better.

She strolled into the main room, picked up the envelope,

thought about it, then didn't open it. Instead she came back to him and put her arms around his neck. "Let's play masseuse," she said in a husky growl, nuzzling him.

They opened the windows, letting the ocean's sounds and salty odors drift indoors. She undressed him slowly, then peeled out of her own clothes. Placing him in their favorite chair again, she stood behind him and gave him a slow facial: her fingers moving lightly over his eyes, forehead, and mouth.

"Relax," she whispered. "I'm your masseuse making her weekly house call. Your wife is always here in the house, watching, and until now we haven't had sex. But today she's gone. So I undressed, too. And let you watch my little striptease. And now we're alone. Just relax."

"Sorry," he told her, laughing. "Impossible."

"Yes, I can see that," she said, coming around the chair with a smile and kneeling between his legs. "My beautiful dark client can't relax. He needs professional help. He needs release. So now he should fuck my mouth."

Expertly, with just the right pressure in her grip, masturbating him, she slipped the head of his cock in her mouth. Her mouth was a little oven, and the rhythmic strokes brought him off quickly. When he finished and sagged in the chair, she couldn't wait for her turn, so wedged in beside him and nudged him out.

She tasted like ocean salt and a sour honey. Even as she moved against his tongue, though, she kept up the story line: the empty house, her husband away on business, the visiting masseur, a rub-down evolving into sex. When he finished, her downy cunt hair was wet and plastered down.

Cal stretched out on the floor wondering if some real masseur had done her. He also wanted to know about the strange guy in the business suit and the mysterious envelope, but told himself, No, hell, why do I want to know her secrets? I won't ask. Fuck her. Literally.

She stood by the window looking out to sea.

"Let's get out of here," she suddenly said. "Let's drive down to Danger Point and stay with Enid at the ranch. The party's down there tomorrow, but we'll go early. She'll love it if we just show up."

"Who's Enid?"

"An old family friend. Let's do it. We'll have lunch on the way. And we'll wear jeans. Nothing fancy for the next two days."

She came over and pulled him upright.

He was playing by Ellen's rules, but didn't care.

5

n the old Jeep they drove out the N1 toward the northeast, then turned into the coastal mountains. Old Huguenot villages appeared along with pastel fields of wildflowers. A fish eagle sailed over an orchard of trees heavy with blossoms. As they went into the foothills the houses grew larger and more severe: the elegance of rich farms and vineyards. With its Dutch Cape architecture each house wore its white-faced gables like bibs: prim starched pilgrims, each farmhouse, standing up straight and pious in the landscape. Landed wealth: a foreign, curious phenomenon to Cal, and something that stirred up a vague hostility in him.

They passed a white church in an arbor of giant oaks. In the shadow of its steeple stood a cluster of believers decked out in dark suits and silk dresses for a wedding or funeral. The sturdy bourgeois: children in their arms, the seasons ticking in their veins, labor and harvest in their stubborn theologies. Not his sort. He knew them as sanctimonious bastards with pride, dirt, and savings accounts. No trespassers allowed. Play it straight or keep out.

Under the eye of the camera, he knew, their faces turned to milk and nothingness.

Rolling green foothills arrived, then valley after valley of lush vineyards: the grapevines neatly staked, the rows clean, all of it aglow in sunlight. A warm January day, the middle of the Cape summer.

He and Ellen talked about Enid, who had once, long ago, been her father's mistress. "Watch out," she warned him. "Enid's a hell of a flirt. Old as she is. She has this big place on the sea: a ranch with, um, horses, cats, books, videos, art, and rusted farm implements."

She turned to catch him looking into her denim shirt. "Hey, give it a rest," she said, and she gave him her slutty laugh.

They drove into a high grassland of electric green, mountain cliffs all around them.

"Before I was born there were Cape lions in these mountains," she said, driving. "But they became extinct, so I never saw one. Yet I miss them. Sounds ridiculous, I know, but it's so sad."

Wistful and somehow far away, Ellen had a wild, curious strength—a thing he somehow knew, but couldn't put into words.

On a road high above the sea as they turned eastward there stood a pile of smooth stones fashioned into a crude shrine. It bore a wooden sign with crude, hand-painted words: THE CHURCH OF THE NEW ZION. Standing beside it was a gnarled black man with a Bible in one hand and an umbrella in the other, an umbrella decorated with bright plastic strips, bangles, and pictures cut from faded magazines.

"Muti," Ellen remarked as they passed. "A medicine man and his little roadside church."

"What's he got? A magic umbrella?"

"If it keeps the rain off him with all those holes in it, it would be a miraculous umbrella," she answered, smiling.

They entered a gated ranch: high grass, views of the sea, horses in the fields.

"Did you bring your camera?" she asked.

"Sure," he said. "With strangers I hide behind cameras."

The house appeared, an unexpected and oversized igloo: a white scoop of ice cream melting on the green landscape. As they approached he leaned out the window and made two quick exposures.

Enid met them on the lawn, sweeping out to greet them. She was full of affectations and lots of "dahlings," but Cal liked her. They managed introductions, admiring each other's clothing.

"Leather—and a nice yellow," she said, stroking his jacket, and her breathy voice trailed off into a guttural sound, an amused growl.

The interior of her house was an extravagence of curves: no straight walls, the corners rounded, the doorways swept up in plaster arches, balconies curving out to offer sea views. Enid herself was costumed in a Lagerfeld jacket, red, with tight jeans and an assortment of beads.

"Oh god, sit down! Please, dahlings, anywhere! Let's get drunk! What a season this has been! Half the horses decided to get sick!"

This spouting, of course, was a cover, and Ellen dutifully rolled her eyes and acknowledged it with laughter. As Enid poured out the gin in reckless measurements, she assessed Cal, and he knew that her observations were shutter-speed quick. As she stirred up drinks, he stepped back, raised his camera, and clicked off shots of the room, the two women, and the balcony views. Enid seemed to love him for it.

"Yes, dear, please, take it all in! This house is a curative for every-one's ills! Don't you feel it? Here, sit beside me. Where'd you find this creature, Ellen? God, look at the thighs on this beast!"

They drank and laughed at her performance. He made another exposure. Everything was white with splashes of color—done with a designer's care. On the table beside their tumblers of gin was a tarot deck.

The old woman started immediately on her dead husbands. "I knew they were doomed, dahlings, not that I wanted them to go, but they were all elderly, don't you see? Although I didn't marry a single one of them for his money, no, I'm not that sort, I married strictly for love each time and nursed them all to the bloody end!"

"You wore them out," Ellen commented.

"Sexually, you mean? Well, mind you, I never refused any of them, but if I helped them toward their graves with a bit of sexual exercise, it was their own lewd gluttony, nothing more or less."

"Enid was a sex machine," Ellen said, grinning. "Her husbands always left their calm and ladylike wives for her, though, so, yes, it was, um, their own damn fault."

"Now, Cal, believe this, dahling, death has an aura about it," Enid said more solemnly. "It gets in the air before it actually happens. As though the ghost gets all restless inside the body!"

"Don't go mystical," Ellen told her, smirking.

"I can't help it, dahling! Death is quite moving. I mean, I was holding Terry's hand. That's the first husband, the one in the export business—which is to say he bought and sold anything that moved through the shipping lanes of this world. Trinkets. Shiploads of stolen refrigerators. Bananas. Once he bought the entire pineapple crop of Zambia. Another time he had these six lorries filled with fertilizer moving all over Africa from one country to the next. They started out for Kampala, but he had a better offer in Kenya, so directed them there. Then Lusaka phoned, so he switched again. Spent all his profit on petrol being wonderfully indecisive!"

"You were holding his hand?" Cal prompted her.

"Oh, dahling, yes, the life went out of him, and I felt it go. He became a husk, and I held this hand, this empty hand, and he was quite gone. What are you anyway? A Scorpio, I'll wager."

"Good guess," Cal admitted.

"Not a guess at all. I'm psychic—especially around dark, good-looking men."

"She's coming on to you," Ellen warned him.

"Of course, naturally! We should get drunk and take a nice bath together; how about it?"

"I'm going riding," Ellen announced, laughing and rising.

"Oh, see, he's a definite Scorpio!" Enid said, grabbing Cal's hand. "And your life line, dahling, goes all the way around your wrist! And look at that heart line! Oh, you cruel bastard! Ellen, look, he's going to pull your heart out of your pretty chest!"

"He already has. And I'm going to find myself a mount while there's still a bit of daylight."

"Take the gray and don't fall off," Enid instructed her. "You've had a nice stiff gin, you remember!"

When Ellen departed, Enid sat back and smiled at Cal. She was seventy, perhaps a great deal more: thin-lipped, hawklike, with a nervous charm that quickly settled into seriousness as it did now.

"Now, dahling, don't you want me to tell your fortune?"

"I'm not a believer," he assured her.

"Ah, yes, I can see that. And I could use your palm or the tarot, but all that's just mechanism. I can see a great deal without any of that. For instance, on the way here you passed a *yurt*—a little shelter, the church of the Muti."

"It's there on the road," he said, grinning. "You know very well that we passed by it."

"Yes, but you felt something as you passed. A stirring. You had this emotion you don't understand, and, well, dahling, the Muti brought it forward in you, didn't he?"

Cal sipped his gin, not denying it. But how, he wondered, did she know this?

"Tell me about Ellen," he urged her, changing the subject.

"Ah, such a love. Won't she tell you about herself?"

"Not really," he admitted.

"So there's only sex between you?"

Cal shrugged. That was enough, he wanted to say. Yet it wasn't.

"She's very special to many of us," Enid offered. "She's our courage. Can I explain this to you? You're not political in the least, are you?"

"Back home I vote Democrat," he said, smiling.

"There, yes, quite so. Americans and their politics. In the rest of the world the activists take risks, bleed, and often go crazy for politics. Unfortunately, perhaps, we're all in that category here, dahling, and can't help ourselves. It's too much sex, too much wine, and too many strong passions for us. And difficult for you to comprehend, I'd wager."

He sipped his gin, listening.

"You're intrigued with her," Enid continued. "Of course you are, dahling, and no wonder. Her lovers undoubtedly feel—well, her depth. They detect it, yet few of them know exactly what it is. For that matter I don't fully understand her myself, and I've known her since her childhood. She was always stronger than the rest of us. And fearless. We admire her and we want to be fearless, too, although we just can't."

He kept his silence until Enid said, "I'll make a prediction: When your time with her is finished, you'll be someone else entirely."

"That's true of all affairs," he offered, trying a little worldly wisdom of his own.

"Hm, yes, true, but now you are going to find what we call the *onverwacht,* the unexpected. It's everywhere for you now. It surrounds you. And that's what you're feeling."

That evening a cool rain arrived, so Enid asked Cal to build up a fire in the hearth. The women set out cold cuts, opened several bottles of wine, and filled his ears with gossip. They spoke openly about how, after Ellen's mother died, the general carried on with Enid for a while. They ended it, Enid said, because General Hofmyr couldn't afford her and because she was too mystical for him.

"So how did you two get to know each other?" Cal asked.

"When Ellen was little, dahling, we had our conspiracies against her father. In those days it was toys and treats, but later on it was political. The general has always been too stuffy for us."

"Also, Enid would talk sex with me," Ellen added. "And, after all, the national sport of South Africa isn't rugby. It's copulation."

"Highest divorce rate in the world, and we're proud of it," Enid said. "And we pride ourselves in knowing exactly who's fucking who, don't we, Ellen, my dear?"

"We're a small and talkative little tribe," Ellen admitted. "And we also talk openly about sex because we usually can't mention the really important matter of race. When that subject comes up, we have to speak in codes and follow all sorts of social courtesies. So what's the dinner topic going to be? Sexual chitchat. And it's always fashionable to have something on the side—and to talk about it within limits. Because there's this great lie hanging around. We have to be candid about our lesser sins."

"Now don't get started, my dear," Enid warned.

"Right. We'll concentrate on tomorrow's party. Is everyone coming?"

"So far as I know," Enid replied. "Including Moppo. Talk about your handsome black man!"

"Oh, do me a great favor, Cal, please. Take lots of photos," Ellen said, touching his sleeve. "Will you? Just be our official photographer? Please?"

"Like group snapshots?"

"If you don't mind."

"Sure. What's the celebration?"

"Just friends getting together," Ellen assured him. "Another party. We do lots of parties because, um, these days you never know."

6

That night in their bedroom Ellen wanted more games.

They played schoolmaster and student.

She reported to his office—the little writing desk in the alcove beside their bed—wearing cotton knee stockings, a short pleated skirt, and a white blouse primly buttoned up. She submitted to punishment for breaking school rules, so he sat her on his lap and gave the upturned palms of her hands a few gentle slaps. Then she stripped down to the knee stockings and asked to receive the rod that her schoolmates had told her so much about.

In all this he was the stern schoolmaster, not Cal.

She smiled and laughed, yet had a faraway look in her eyes, too, as if the fantasy was everything.

Cal tried to keep up with all her instructions. "Bite me," she insisted. "I've been a bad girl and I deserve a rough fuck."

Later they played a threesome with his camera.

"Let's see, it's a movie camera," she asserted, smiling. "I'm the porno queen and you're the cinematographer. You always watch while I screw the hired studs, but tonight it's snowing and you offer to drive me home. We're in Stockholm. There's a heavy snowfall and, yes, there, rub it in a little circle just there. Anyway, we go to my apartment and I ask if you don't want to fuck me and you answer, yes, sure, but you also want to film whatever we do. Some, um, there, do it in slow motion. Perfect. Are you filming? Slow motion, ah, freeze frame, good, now slow motion again."

When she finished she rode him to orgasm, then rolled off. He stretched out on the coverlet of the bed, groaning, "No more. You've used me up. Finished."

"There's a great silence in a Stockholm winter," she said drowsily. "The silence plays with your head. Then, sometimes, the sound of a distant teacup brings you back. You return to your normal complicated awareness. Know what I mean?"

"Hm," he replied, and he asked her why she had commissioned her father's portrait.

"Oh, it's a long story."

"Tell me," he urged her, knowing she didn't want to.

"In my teen years I was a raging liberal," she began, sighing. "Demonstrations and petitions, that sort of thing. I was also dating interracial. The general wasn't for apartheid, not at all, but when I dated black guys, he went a little bonkers. I had to become very secretive. Because of the general. Now it suits me to have myself identified with his military career and his more conservative views. I'd like to present the portrait to his old regiment someday soon—and have my own photo in the newspapers doing it."

"Then the portrait's really for you?"

"Absolutely," she admitted. "The general's far too modest and too tight with his money to want such a thing for himself. Here, give me your big toe."

Cal obliged and she made use of it, moving it onto her clit.

"There, see," she told him. "You still have a part standing and you've discovered the real me."

7

The next day around noon the guests arrived, more than twenty of them in several vehicles.

Ellen greeted each one—a tall black woman, eight black men, an old Indian gentleman, the rest whites—and kept signaling to Cal to take photos of everyone in groups of three or four. She introduced him as the famous American photographer, and one of the Brits, Neville, professed to know Cal's work.

They smiled and posed for his camera, yet they were a somber group, academics wearing earnest expressions and whispering in small clusters around the house and terraces. Enid circulated with a tray of drinks—dahlings! hello!—but couldn't stir up a party mood.

Ellen moved from one group to another, too, touching everyone, smiling, and joining their discussions. As she moved around she energized them: nods, guarded laughter occasionally, then bursts of renewed conversation. Cal saw a new Ellen: the hostess, clearly, and in some curious way the centerpiece of the occasion. Ellen and the tall black woman exchanged fierce hugs and kissed each other's cheeks. Later, Cal went over and introduced himself for the second time. The woman had big hair, a tight red dress, and spiked heels that put her two inches taller than Cal. One of her gold ear bangles was held together by a delicate strip of soiled adhesive tape.

Maybe, he decided, she's from some escort service. A fine ass on a willowy frame. He decided to hit on her, lightly.

"Ever been on the Blue Train?" he asked, starting up.

"No, not really. The Blue Train's for diplomats and such."

"But suppose I bought tickets and you came along as my personal secretary?" he suggested.

She gave him a smirk and a throaty laugh. "If I traveled on the Blue Train I'd call attention to myself," she answered. "Even if I was in your hire, they might detain me. And my papers aren't in such good order, so anything could happen."

"Because of the pass laws? Would it be illegal, then?"

"Ah, screw illegal. I don't mind illegal. Even my skin is bloody illegal, isn't it?"

"So if I paid you well, you might risk it?"

"I might. In a posh hotel or nightclub nobody says anything about a white tourist and his black escort, so the Blue Train might be like that. You're a cheeky sort. Are you actually asking me to go?"

"Not at the moment. What's your name?"

"Pola. I work in water resources."

"Good," he said, smiling.

The afternoon, after lunch, eased into a soft inebriation so that the groups seemed less intense and more friendly. Cal, satisfied that a single roll of 35 mm film was enough, stopped taking pictures and drank, in turn, a nice Riesling, some grappa, and a bit of pike brandy. Then he met Moppo, clearly an important figure in the group: the only black wine master in the region, he learned, and a remarkable physical specimen. Moppo had a muscled, easy grace with a thin waist, wide shoulders, and biceps straining against his short sleeves. His hands were twice the size of Cal's, rough and black with gray calluses and shiny pink nails. His shirt was Ralph Lauren denim and he wore jeans and snakeskin boots, so he looked like a prosperous Texas rancher, a man of the soil no longer required to work it with his own strength. Cal listened while Moppo told how his workers had recently removed the stones from the fields, giant stones used to reflect the sun's heat in the cooler months so the grapes would ripen faster. He heard, too, how the Petrus was added in a certain amount to the Loudenne this year to achieve the Merlot and how, in Moppo's opinion, this would be a vintage year because of the right amounts of rain, dew, and sun. A boring, technical sort of man, Cal decided, trying to impress others with his station in life.

Around the house before supper the talk ranged from something called Wits to Helena Bonham Carter to AIDS among the mine workers.

Neville, the Brit, tended to make speeches. "Eighty years ago we were a beloved people throughout the world," he said, once. His listeners consisted of Pola and the old Indian—who might have been deaf. "President Kruger was welcomed in Europe as if he'd established a paradise," he went on. "General Jan Smuts was the spiritual father of the League of Nations—and wrote, in fact, the bloody preamble to the charter of the U.N. We had moral leadership! And it was our belief in fairness and coexistence that started us off!"

Cal excused himself, moved away, and found Enid.

"Dahling! Having a good time?"

"These are serious people," he complained.

"So true. And they improve very little as they get drunk."

"Where's Ellen?"

Enid couldn't say. As he looked for her, he stopped for a cup of espresso with Pola.

They talked for a while, then she told him a story.

"When I was a girl in the Christian school, some police came with their fiberglass quirts," she said, turning the coffee cup in her long fingers. "They whipped two of our teachers in the hallway. One of my schoolmates threw a stone at their lorry, so they also beat her. When someone is hit by a quirt, ah, it makes a white streak on the black skin, then the white streak opens up, it sort of flowers, it opens like this, and the blood comes out."

"This is your elementary school?"

"I was, ah, twelve years old. One of the policemen questioned me about my political beliefs. He took his quirt and raised the front of my dress with it while he did this."

Cal fell silent.

"Yes, I was once a very good Zulu girl in the Christian school in Durban. I even attended one year at university. But, ah, no scholarship and too many boyfriends. That year I went to demonstrations and then, well, to say the truth, I became afraid. Our friends were in detention. But you don't want to hear all this."

He assured her that he did, yet didn't. Eventually he moved away, where Moppo stopped him. He wanted his photograph with his new truck, so Cal found his camera and they went outdoors. In the last light of day Moppo posed with his snakeskin boot on the bumper of a shiny Dodge Ram.

At super they toasted names Cal didn't know: many toasts, some of them tearful, so that he knew these were people no longer with them. Toward midnight Ellen led him up to their bedroom. She slipped out of her jeans—no panties, as promised—and asked if he had taken photos of everybody.

"I just shot one roll—thirty-six exposures—but, yeah, I got everybody and several of Moppo and his new truck."

"I appreciate it, Cal, really, but do me a favor, will you?"

"You're doing me one right now," he said, admiring her.

"Like it?"

"Love it. What's the favor?"

"Keep the roll of film and give it to me later back in Cape Town."

"Sure. And c'mere," he said, grinning.

She strolled toward him, but remained less playful than he expected. "Something else," she said. "I can't drive back with you. I'll come, um, a day later. And if you don't mind, love, would you check into a hotel instead of going back to my place?"

Let her have her intrigue, he decided. Maybe someone else was on her dance card. "I'll check into the Mount Nelson," he offered. "When do you think you'll join me?"

"Why don't we say lunch day after tomorrow?"

He assumed she did have someone else, possibly the guy who showed up in her place or somebody here at the party. He wondered ever so briefly if Pola might be available.

"Sounds good," he replied. "Lunchtime in two days. Anything else?"

"Oh, I hope so," she said, finally crawling onto the bed and once more propping herself on a mound of pillows. She summoned him with a crooked finger.

"Tell you what," he said, undressing and joining her. "Why don't we play Cal and Ellen this time?"

"We did that on the train. Let's do jailbait instead."

"Jailbait?" he asked, manufacturing a smile and moving against her. He covered his disappointment by kissing her shoulder.

"You're the warden and I'm your prisoner. You demand favors of me while I'm wearing handcuffs," she said, and she arched herself and held her hands above her head.

Although he submitted he felt annoyed.

On the train, he clearly remembered, they had played artist and model.

8

Cal was assigned to drive back to Cape Town with the talkative Brit, Neville, who started right away on Americans.

"Naturally, Americans have heard of South Africa and its problems, but then all news and information is much the same to them. It comes over the telly, gets a nod, then onto the next item. Michael Jackson's sex: Now there's a burning issue. Or what Marlon or Liz or some randy politician is doing. The world's real horrors sort of blend into the show biz. Americans are a loud and trivial people, as trivial as rock music."

Cal slumped in anger, watching the passing scenery and trying to think of some clever retort, but managed only, "Everybody's happy to have us as the world's policemen. When there's dirty work, everyone wants the Yanks to go clean it up, right?"

"Yes, but Americans are like tourists for the most part," Neville went on. "They wander in and out of countries taking culture samples. They're nomads. The passing caravan. They never actually understand or feel anyone else's problems, do they? They just want the world to behave itself—and they believe they can throw money at people's differences and make everything jolly."

They drove on the N1, traffic whizzing by. Neville's Toyota had the odor of leather and pipe tobacco.

After a few more miles, though, Neville revealed his true discontent. "I suppose you're shagging Ellen?" he asked with as much fake indifference as he could muster.

"Oh, sure," Cal replied casually, then he allowed the silence to gather between them. "Actually, Neville, she loves Americans. We fuck like cowboys. At least I do."

It was the meanest thing he could imagine to say.

9

Cal's windows at the Mount Nelson Hotel had views of Lion's Head and the edge of Table Mountain, then, from another angle, the sunny waters of the south Atlantic.

He spent the next day on the telephone with his widowed mother, his answering service, his broker, and the secretary of a prospective client in Atlanta, but after the telephone voices ended a gnawing loneliness set in. He wanted Ellen's body and presence, and although he was scheduled to fly back to the States he wanted to stay. He cursed himself for coming back to the city without her, for not knowing about her friends or business, and for not even knowing Enid's last name—although, of course, Enid had worn several last names, never mind which one the phone company might currently have listed at Danger Point.

He paced around the hotel room. Her lovers, Enid had said, using the plural. And her courage. What did he know about Ellen except her abandon in bed? And wasn't that enough—and the sum of what had been between them? When she went into orgasm, she raised her head slightly, then slammed it back onto the pillow. They used each other like narcotics. Bang away and thanks. Good sex and good-bye. Yet the old satisfactions somehow weren't enough, and an unnamed yearning kept washing over him.

Danger Point. He wasn't even sure where the hell it was.

In the afternoon he took a walk around the hotel's grounds and garden, then strolled downhill through the Botanical Gardens to the city. He picked up a newspaper, but tossed it away, unread, in a wire basket. He wondered if she'd consider flying back to the States with him. He thought about all her games. Little brother. The silent snow of Stockholm.

He slept badly that night, waking for long periods. A fierce wind came up, laying seige to the hotel. He imagined the ocean out there: giant whitecaps in a black night.

The next morning, tired and distracted, he had coffee in his room, then made early lunch plans hoping Ellen would soon arrive. He paced around thinking about entrapments. If I'm a little obsessed with her, he told himself, I should be careful.

Just after ten o'clock that morning he stood at his window in his shirt and shorts, one sock on, when the phone rang.

Neville's voice was cold and brittle.

"Don't say my name on the phone," Neville instructed him. "This must be very quick, but you need to know. Ellen's dead. So is Enid. So is Moppo and Pola. A car crash last night east of Brensmark."

Cal sat down heavily on the windowsill.

"The report," Neville went on, his voice breaking. "The report is that their bodies burned up in the crash. But that's always the story to avoid autopsies, isn't it? That's always the convenient lie they tell."

"Who do you mean?" Cal managed.

"Who do I mean? The death squads. Who the hell do you think I mean, you dumb prick?"

10

Cal rented a car, bought an elaborate road map, and started
driving into the wine country toward a small town called
Brensmark. Although he didn't fully understand why, he meant to
hurry to the site of the wreck. Inside him was a cold shadow, a new
presence that took away most rational thought.

The narrow mountain highway beyond Stellenbosch twisted
through a series of dark glades, a shadowland where even in the
bright summer day a blue pall settled in the valleys. The inhabitants
of the glades—viewed from his car window as he slowed down in
the turns—were light-skinned and mysterious, a people in the
no-man's-land of a mixed race, and for Cal, he felt, the glades bore
some of the atmosphere of the Deep South in America, the scraggly
byways and stopovers of, say, Tennessee or Kentucky, where smoke
and mist settle in the low spots and where thin dogs lurk beside
rusted junkyards, ramshackle houses, and leaning barns. Occasionally the curves of the road opened up into wider meadows, and set
back in stands of timber or alongside rocky streams, Cal glimpsed
large stone houses or another gabled farm mansion, never exactly

elegant, where some landowner in his winery or farm looked out over his feudal domain. The scattered hovels, he knew, belonged to farm workers—farms replete with those scrawny, long-legged chickens pecking in the dust, those inedible-looking birds common over the whole continent. The hovels said clearly, look, poor folks here: water spigots in the yards, no screens on the windows, sad mules, work, Jesus, and early death.

Then arcades of overhanging boughs blotted out the sun as he drove by forests of pine and hardwood that turned the day to quicksilver. In the hairpin turns he stole quick glances into that netherworld of shadowed glades, and it became his own little horror movie: the dark wood, down and down.

He passed through the sleepy little Huguenot town of Brensmark, then kept going east. Not far away at the edge of another forest, the burnt-out husk of the Jeep lay against a tree off the shoulder of the road, its front bashed in, its doors open like charred wings. An immense cottonwood tree nearby sent out its airy white particles on the afternoon breeze, adorning the blackened roof of the vehicle.

Cal parked beside a road flare. A uniformed policeman waved traffic around the scene.

Taking his little Minox out of his gear, Cal walked toward the wreckage. Out of the forest came two men, the largest of them with a walkie-talkie, waving, and calling, "Hold on, please! No photos!"

Cal kept walking toward the wreck until both men intercepted him. Both wore tailored khaki suits, not unlike the one worn by Steyn, the man Cal had met at Ellen's cliffside house.

"You from a newspaper?" the big man barked at him.

"No, just curious," Cal answered.

"Then put your camera away and move on! No photographs!"

The remains of the Jeep sat in a circle of scorched ground. Seeing it, Cal fought for control. The searing heat, he kept thinking. Her body burned up, gone. He trudged back to his rented car as those delicate white particles from the cottonwood settled on him in penitent silence.

As he put his camera away, a Mercedes limo pulled up. A young army sergeant quickly jumped out to open the rear door with a salute, then, slowly, the old man emerged: General Hofmyr, somehow older, wearing his green garden smock and rubber boots. He saw the wreckage immediately, then hurriedly looked away, focusing his gaze on the treetops.

Cal made his way toward the group that formed: the general, his driver, the two men in khaki, the traffic cop. Introductions and information were exchanged before he reached them, then the old man raised his eyes to Cal.

"The portrait photographer," Cal added, after offering his name, and the general looked at him absently, struggling for recognition, then finally nodded his head.

"Yes, oh yes," the old man said with a rasp. "Yes, my boy. And we won't be needing that picture now, will we?" With that he turned and shuffled toward the wreckage.

The acknowledgment, though, allowed Cal to linger, and he joined the others. The burnt Jeep seemed at rest against the trunk of an old oak tree, its chassis charred, yet undented. The left front fender and bumper were missing. The rear tires were flat, and the petrol tank had blown, so that an explosion and fire had obviously originated at the rear of the vehicle. The seats had been removed with the occupants. A sickening odor stayed on: petrol and—what? Cal didn't want to think about it.

Those white cottonwood particles floated down like fog.

The old general shuffled slowly around the wreckage, his eyes clear and observant. He knew. And he spoke to himself softly, his voice dry and feeble, although Cal moved close enough to overhear.

"I told her," he said in a soft rasp. "I told her a thousand times."

11

Once, lying in bed together, not more than a week ago, Cal remembered, Ellen talked about the wildflowers.

When the Ice Age descended millions of years ago, she said, moving down from the polar cap to cover Europe in its flow, slicing the Alps into matterhorns then freezing northern Africa in its onslaught, the Cape was spared. Because the Ice Age didn't reach this far south, she explained, five thousand species of flora were saved and the tip of the continent became a kingdom of wildflowers unlike any place on earth.

Now she was buried on a hillside in view of a rich canopy of growth that dazzled the countryside; the foothills of the coastal mountains had turned to flame for her, and the meadows became bright embers in the morning sunrise. Around the gravesite tall red blooms moved like trembling fingers in the slight breeze, so that Cal asked a young black woman standing nearby what they were called. Wild watsonia. From his vantage point Cal could view both the mountains and sea: a white beach lay like the crook of a shining arm, holding back the surf, and in a faraway crease of the mountains a cluster of slate-covered roofs presented themselves to the hazy sunlight.

He estimated the crowd at the funeral at more than three thousand, mostly blacks, mostly young, with dozens of those grim-faced men in tailored khaki suits—the security force—moving through and around the cemetery.

He saw no one he recognized from Enid's party: not Neville, not the old Indian gentleman, no one.

Hunched over in the only chair beside the casket, the old general looked small and beaten.

A leader of the Reformed Church, a portly white man in a robe trimmed with crimson, offered a long prayer, then an old black woman surrounded by girls in berets who raised their clenched fists, spoke at length, saying, once, "With so many whites we were always standing at the gate, but with Ellen we were always home and inside the house straightaway!" While the crowd responded with amens, a young man with a thick cowlick of blond hair stepped up and tried to lead a song, but his voice broke, and the girls in berets picked up the tune and came to his rescue.

Cal watched as that cold shadow stirred inside him. He thought of yesterday's newspaper, where some friend of the family had been quoted as saying that police versions of the accident were "probably true." In a competing newspaper there was no mention of either the accident or funeral arrangements, not even a modest obituary.

After an hour he moved with the crowd toward the bottom of the hill, wildflowers all around them, then a dusty road opened up, a road lined with cars, old buses, and a few rickety lorries. In that silent file of mourners Cal saw Tom Steyn and moved toward him, pushing through until he was close enough to call out.

"Can you talk with me?" Cal pleaded as they were jostled together by the crowd.

"About what?" Steyn answered sternly, though once again he blushed red. He knew.

"Please," said Cal, and he held on to Steyn's sleeve until at last he relented.

"Yes, all right, I'll come to your hotel," Steyn told him.

"Do you know which hotel?"

"Of course. Four o'clock today in the bar, if that suits you."

Cal thanked him as the movement of the crowd separated them again. For a moment he stood by himself, mourners passing by. The sun bore down on his shoulders, and his shadow was thrown with the others, yet it wasn't his shadow. His real shadow, he felt, was locked inside him, cold and stupid.

12

'll not contact you again after this, Mr. Vega, and if you make an effort to contact me, I'll avoid you. Officially, you could be a great bother to everyone. It won't be personal with me. On the contrary. I'll tell others that you're an American tourist pestering a detective about a delicate matter—and that he's a very busy man who hasn't time for you. Understand?"

Cal nodded. They sat in a secluded booth of dark wood while a lone waiter stood across the room talking on the phone.

Steyn's crimson blush came and went, making Cal wonder if this coloring served as a kind of lie detector.

"This was entirely a security matter," Steyn went on, heaving a sigh. "The case is now closed and will never be reopened. The bodies, as you probably know, were cremated after being badly burned in the wreck. There was no autopsy and no medical report beyond that. There's a one-page traffic report on the accident, nothing more."

They turned their drinks in their hands.

"You knew her only for a short time, Mr. Vega, and you didn't know her very well. I understand you met her up in Jo'burg while working on a portrait of her father, then came down here with her on the Blue Train—sharing the same compartment. Cruel as this might sound, she probably had some use for you. I've personally known the general for many years. His father and my father and all that. And I've known Ellen most of her life. She was someone you fancied you were using for sex, I'll wager, but I don't want to presume. In truth, she was a clever woman who never made a move without a practical and political motive."

"I loved Ellen," Cal insisted.

"No, you didn't," said the detective with a short, harsh laugh.

As the man flushed red at this assertion, they both sipped their drinks.

"There's the Civil Cooperation Bureau," Steyn began again. "You've probably never heard of it. It's a secret army unit. And Ellen and her friends ranked high on their annoyance list."

"You sound as though you don't really care for them," Cal ventured.

"We all hate the bloody fuckers, but there they are. But see here, Mr. Vega, we're a nation of informants, aren't we? We're worse than the Irish in that way. Spying and telling on one another. Since somebody's probably watching us right this minute, I'll have to file a report by way of covering myself, don't you see? And if later you repeat anything I've said to you in confidence, I'll turn against you. I'll say you're a bloody liar. Because I'm a family man. Two children. My father worked most of his life as a mine guard, and we were poor. And if my job often shows me the worst of this country, I'm still a proud professional, believe me, and I hate murder or seeing anyone get away with it."

Cal believed him.

"I was a friend to Ellen and tried to help. That packet I left at her house that day we first met, well, it was a bit of information I tried to provide. Information and a warning, Mr. Vega, because I knew the danger."

The detective gazed around the empty bar as the color gathered in his cheeks. He was trying hard to be patient with Cal.

"If someone in this country ever advocates violence," he went on, "they're considered a terrorist, no two ways about it. And we want our terrorists dead—same as you—as a matter of convenience. When you turn on your tap, you don't care where the water comes from. When you switch on your telly, you don't want to know the physics of it. You just want things to work. Convenient like. Same as we do, you Americans want your terrorists and criminals out of sight, preferably dead. But cold-blooded murder sticks in the throat no matter who does it. Even if the state does it, it's bloody business, so take my advice: Buy yourself an airline ticket and leave. Then try to live with circumstances."

Cal nodded and finished his whiskey.

"You didn't know her," Steyn went on. "She was dangerous, and you should've been afraid. Me, I'm afraid all the time. Because accidents can happen to any of us. Even having this little conversation with you has its risks and could present me with a whole set of bloody damned problems."

Although the detective spoke quietly he had turned crimson.

"By the way, those photos you made for Ellen," he went on. "You didn't give them to Neville or anyone else, did you?"

"No, they're here in my pocket. The undeveloped roll."

"They're meant for me. Will you please let me have them?"

Cal hesitated.

"Ellen was looking for the informant at her party. I was the one who would inspect the photos and hope to tell her the informant's identity. Of course it's already too late for her and the others, but I might save somebody else's life if I can make an identification."

Cal handed over the roll of film. "I suppose I have to trust you," he said.

They both slid out of the booth. The detective managed a grim smile. "Please, Mr. Vega. You're a long way from Texas. You're on my turf. I know what I'm telling you. Go home."

13

The midsummer heat of Austin.

From the window of his studio in the hill country just west of the city, Cal watched his mother squinting beneath a wide straw hat as she watered the rosebushes and sipped iced tea. Her absent gaze was far away, so the hard stream from the hose splashed a hole beside one of her favorite bushes. His mother had stayed with him for a few weeks, moving around in her distracted way, more feeble than he liked to think about, yet she gave him companionship and something to occupy his thoughts when he wasn't working.

He had just come back from doing a portrait in Atlanta. His subject, a society woman, exuded a fake effervescence, and was the sort of woman he called formerly cute.

While in Atlanta he picked up another woman, a divorcée with a deep sunburn who worked with men in hardhats on a road crew. In his hotel room, stripped for his inspection, her arms and face were bright red while the rest of her body gave off a sad, pale glow.

They fumbled around on the bed until she suggested a game of make-believe. She wanted to be a stripper, she said, and he could be the nightclub owner visiting her dressing room. She went on with this until he asked her to leave, making her so angry that he thought they might have a fistfight.

His efforts, recently, had become comedy without laughter.

Now he stood in a blast of noonday heat on his deck. He drank a salty dog. To the west lay the rocky Texas hill country. It reminded him of the flatland viewed from the windows of the Blue Train and had become his own little arid karoo. When he looked out on it these days—he had come back from South Africa more than a year ago—he felt that shadow stirring inside him, a dim presence nobody else could possibly know about or detect.

South Africa, of course, was in every newscast: Mandela released from prison, the pass laws abolished, so much. It was history, detached and unreal, the abstractions of politics, yet the private history down in his own sad darkroom, that hurt: Ellen's face and body, the curve of her breast as it sloped away from her underarm, the soft vagina that returned his kisses with its gentle nudge, the sly glance. He missed her, missed the man he once was, and somehow missed, he knew, a great chance in his life, so that he felt dull and stupid. I was stupid, he told himself: stupid, stupid, stupid.

Author Biographies

TSAURAH LITZKY

Tsaurah Litzky is the author of the poetry collection *Baby on the Water*. She teaches erotic writing and erotic literature at the New School in New York. She has been a six-time contributor to the Best American Erotica series. Her apartment is directly under the Brooklyn Bridge, where she can see the Statue of Liberty—symbol of free women everywhere—each night when she eats her dinner.

GREG BOYD

A painter and printmaker as well as a writer, Greg Boyd has published ten books, most recently *The Double (Doppelangelganger): An Annotated Novel*. His work as a writer includes collections of prose poems, essays, short stories, and a translation of Charles Baudelaire's novella *La Fanfarlo*. His photo collages and prints have been exhibited and published all over the world. His story "Horny" was published in the first edition of *The Best American Erotica*, and has been a reader favorite since. He lives in northern California.

WILLIAM HARRISON

William Harrison is the author of screenplays, travel pieces, two collections of short stories, and eight novels. Harrison was an English professor at the University of Arkansas when he wrote the "The Roller Ball Murders," "Mountains of the Moon," and "A Shining Season," which became legendary movies. His last five novels, including the most recent, *The Blood Latitudes,* have African settings. Another of his novels, *Three Hunters,* is currently in film production.

About the Editor

Susie Bright is the editor of the bestselling Best American Erotica and Herotica series, and the author of some of the most influential books in contemporary sexual politics, including *Mommy's Little Girl: On Sex, Motherhood, Porn, and Cherry Pie*. She hosts the weekly audio show "In Bed with Susie Bright" on Audible.com, and performs and teaches creative writing and sex education throughout the world. She lives in northern California with her partner and daughter, and can be found at www.susiebright.com.